LIFE IS OUT THERE...

And it's coming to a planet near you!

How will we know the human race has been infiltrated by beings from another world? "Galactic Chest" and "He Knew All the Answers" are good examples of what to look for.

In "The Awful Weapon" we see yet another example of how political maneuvering often backfires and "Navy Day" shares the continual antagonistic shenanigans of Army vs. Navy.

Murder and mayhem exist even in the outskirts of space, whether it's brought about by man as in "Secret of the Burning Finger," or by aliens as in "The Survivors."

And who, or what, is included under the banner of God's Children? Maybe "All Jackson's Children" will shed some light on the subject...

TABLE OF CONTENTS

SCIENCE FICTION GEMS

Volume 5

CLIFFORD D. SIMAK
and others

ARMCHAIR FICTION
PO Box 4369, Medford, Oregon 97504

For *more information about Armchair Books and products, visit our website at…*

www.armchairfiction.com

Or email us at…

armchairfiction@yahoo.com

Galactic Chest

By CLIFFORD D. SIMAK

In the long run, every person, every race, has to solve its own problems. But if some of the little details that obscure the big issues could be cleared away...

I HAD just finished writing the daily community chest story, and each day I wrote that story I was sore about it; there were plenty of punks in the office who could have ground out that kind of copy. Even the copy boys could have written it and no one would have known the difference; no one ever read it— except maybe some of the drive chairmen, and I'm not even sure about them reading it.

I had protested to Barnacle Bill about my handling the community chest for another year. I had protested loud. I had said: "Now, you know, Barnacle, I been writing that thing for three or four years. I write it with my eyes shut. You ought to get some new blood into it. Give one of the cubs a chance; they can breathe some life into it. Me, I'm all written out on it."

But it didn't do a bit of good. The Barnacle had me down on the assignment book for the community chest, and he never changed a thing once he put it in the book.

I wish I knew the real reason for that name of his. I've heard a lot of stories about how it was hung on him, but I don't think there's any truth in them. I think he got it simply from the way he can hang onto a bar.

I had just finished writing the community chest story and was sitting there, killing time and hating myself, when along came Jo Ann. Jo Ann was the sob sister on the paper; she got some lousy yarns to write, and that's a somber fact. I guess it was because I am of a sympathetic nature, and took pity on her, and let her cry upon my shoulder that we got to know each other so well. By now, of course, we figure we're in love; off and on we talk about getting married, as soon as I snag that foreign correspondent job I've been angling for.

"Hi, kid," I said.

And she says, "Do you know, Mark, what the Barnacle has me down for today?"

"He'd finally ferreted out a one-armed paperhanger," I guessed, "and he wants you to do a feature…"

"It's worse than that," she moans. "It's an old lady who is celebrating her one hundredth birthday."

"Maybe" I said, "she will give you a piece of her birthday cake."

"I don't see how even you can joke about a thing like this," Jo Ann told me. "It's positively ghastly."

Just then the Barnacle let out a bellow for me. So I picked up the community chest story and went over to the city desk.

BARNACLE BILL is up to his elbows in copy; the phone is ringing and he's ignoring it, and for this early in the morning he has worked himself into more than a customary lather. "You remember old Mrs. Clayborne?"

"Sure, she's dead. I wrote the obit on her ten days or so ago."

"Well, I want you to go over to the house and snoop around a bit."

"What for?" I asked. "She hasn't come back, has she?"

"No, but there's some funny business over there. I got a tip that someone might have hurried her a little."

"This time," I told him, "you've out done yourself. You've been watching too many television thrillers."

"I got it on good authority," he said and turned back to his work.

So I went and got my hat and told myself it was no skin off my nose how I spent the day; I'd get paid just the same…

But I was getting a little fed up on some of the wild goose chases to which the Barnacle was assigning not only me, but the rest of the staff as well. Sometimes they paid off; usually, they didn't. And when they didn't, Barnacle had the nasty habit of making it appear that the man he had sent out, not he himself, had dreamed up the chase. His "good authority" probably was no more than some casual chatter of someone next to him at the latest bar he'd honored with his cash.

OLD MRS. CLAYBORNE had been one of the last of the faded gentility, which at one time had graced Douglas Avenue. The family had petered out, and she was the last of them; she had died in a big and lonely house with only a few servants, and a nurse in attendance on her, and no kin close enough to wait out her final hours in person.

It was unlikely, I told myself, that anyone could have profited by giving her an overdose of drugs, or in any otherwise hurrying her death. And even if it were true, there'd be little chance that it could be proved; and that was the kind of story you didn't run unless you had it down in black and white.

I went out to the house on Douglas Avenue. It was a quiet and lovely place, standing in its fenced-in yard among the autumn-colored trees.

There was an old gardener raking leaves, and he didn't notice me when I went up the walk. He was an old man, pottering away and more than likely mumbling to himself, and I found out later that he was a little deaf.

I went up the steps, rang the bell and stood waiting, feeling cold at heart and wondering what I'd say once I got inside. I couldn't say what I had in mind; somehow or other I'd have to go about it by devious indirection.

I needn't have worried; I never got inside.

A maid came to the door.

"Good morning, ma'am," I said. "I am from the *Tribune*. May I come in and talk?"

She didn't even answer; she looked at me for a moment and then slammed the door. I told myself I might have known that was the way it would be.

I TURNED around, went down the steps, and cut across the grounds to where the gardener was working. He didn't notice me until I was almost upon him; when he did see me, his face sort of lit up. He dropped the rake, and sat down on the wheelbarrow. I suppose I was as good an excuse as any for him to take a breather.

"Hello," I said to him.

"Nice day," he said to me.

"Indeed it is."

"You'll have to speak up louder," he told me. "I can't hear a thing you say."

"Too bad about Mrs. Clayborne," I told him.

"Yes, yes," he said. "You live around here? I don't recall your face."

I nodded; it wasn't much of a lie, just twenty miles or so.

"She was a nice old lady. Worked for her almost fifty years. It's a blessing she is gone."

"I suppose it is."

"She was dying hard," he said.

He sat nodding in the autumn sun and you could almost hear his mind go traveling back across those fifty years. I am certain that, momentarily, he'd forgotten I was there.

"Nurse tells a funny story," he said finally, speaking to himself more than he spoke to me. "It might be just imagining. Nurse was tired, you know."

"I heard about it," I encouraged him.

"Nurse left her just a minute and she swears there was something in the room when she came back again. Says it went out the window just as she came in. Too dark to see it good, she says. I told her she was imagining. Funny things happen, though; things we don't know about."

"That was her room," I said, pointing at the house. "I remember, years ago…"

HE CHUCKLED at having caught me in the wrong. "You're mistaken, sonny. It was the corner one; that one over there."

He rose from the barrow slowly and took up the rake again.

"It was good to talk with you," I said. "These are pretty flowers you have. Mind if I walk around and have a look at them."

"Might as well. Frost will get them in a week or so."

So I walked around the grounds, hating myself for what I had to do, and looking at the flowers, working my way closer to the corner of the house he had pointed out to me.

There was a bed of petunias underneath the window and they were sorry looking things. I squatted down and pretended I was admiring them, although all the time I was looking for some evidence that someone might have jumped out the window.

I didn't expect to find it, but I did.

There, in a little piece of soft earth where the petunias had petered out, was a footprint—well, not a footprint, either, maybe, but anyhow a print. It looked something like a duck track—except that the duck that made it would have had to be as big as a good-sized dog.

I squatted on the walk, staring at it and I could feel spiders on my spine. Finally I got up and walked away, forcing myself to saunter when my body screamed to run.

Outside the gate, I *did* run.

I GOT TO a phone as fast as I could, at a corner drugstore, and sat in the booth awhile to get my breathing back to normal before I put in a call to the city desk.

The Barnacle bellowed at me, "What you got?"

"I don't know," I said. "Maybe nothing. Who was Mrs. Clayborne's doctor?"

He told me. I asked him if he knew who her nurse had been, and he asked how the hell should he know so I hung up.

I went to see the doctor and he threw me out.

I spent the rest of the day tracking down the nurse; when I finally found her she threw me out too. So there was a full day's work gone entirely down the drain.

It was late in the afternoon when I got back to the office. Barnacle Bill pounced on me at once. "What you get?"

"Nothing," I told him. There was no use telling him about that track underneath the window. By that time, I was beginning to doubt I'd ever seen it, it seemed so unbelievable.

"How big do ducks get?" I asked him. He growled at me and went back to his work.

I looked at the next day's page in the assignment book. He had me down for the community chest, and: *See Dr. Thomas at Univ.—magnetism.*

"What's this?" I asked. "This magnetism business?"

"Guy's been working on it for years," said the Barnacle. "I got it on good authority he's set to pop with something."

There was that "good authority" again. And just about as hazy as the most of his hot tips.

And anyhow, I don't like to interview scientists. More often than not, they're a crotchety set and are, apt to look down their noses at newspapermen. Ten to one the newspaperman is earning more than they are—and in his own way, more than likely, doing just as good a job and with less fumbling.

CHAPTER TWO

I SAW THAT Jo Ann was getting ready to go home, so I walked over to her and asked her how it went.

"I got a funny feeling in my gizzard, Mark," she told me. "Buy me a drink and I'll tell you all about it."

So we went down to the corner bar and took a booth way in the back.

Joe came over and he was grumbling about business, which was unusual for him. "If it weren't for you folks over at the paper," he said, "I'd close up and go home. That must be what all my customers are doing; they sure ain't coming here. Can you think of anything more disgusting than going straight home from your job?"

We told him that we couldn't, and to show that he appreciated our attitude he wiped off the table—a thing he almost never did.

He brought the drinks and Jo Ann told me about the old lady and her hundredth birthday. "It was horrible. There she sat in her rocking chair in that bare living room, rocking back and forth, gently, delicately, the way old ladies rock. And she was glad to see me, and she smiled so nice and she introduced me all around."

"Well, that was fine," I said. "Were there a lot of people there?"

"Not a soul."

I CHOKED on my drink. "But you said she introduced…"

"She did. To empty chairs."

"Good Lord!"

"They all were dead," she said.

"Now, let's get this straight…"

"She said, 'Miss Evans, I want you to meet my old friend, Mrs. Smith. She lives just down the street. I recall the day she moved into the neighborhood, back in '33. Those were hard times, I tell you.' Chattering on, you know like most old ladies do. And me, standing there and staring at an empty chair, wondering what to do. And, Mark, I don't know if I did right or not, but I said, 'Hello, Mrs. Smith. I am glad to know you.' And do you know what happened then?"

"No," I said. "How could I?"

"The old lady said, just as casually as could be—just conversationally, as if it were the most natural thing in all the world—'You know, Miss Evans, Mrs. Smith died three years ago. Don't you think it's nice she dropped in to see me?'"

"She was pulling your leg," I said. "Some of these old ones sometimes get pretty sly."

"I don't think she was. She introduced me all around; there were six or seven of them, and all of them were dead."

"She was happy, thinking they were there. What difference does it make?"

"It was horrible," said Jo Ann.

So we had another drink to chase away the horror.

JOE STILL was down in the mouth. "Did you ever see the like of it? You could shoot off a cannon in this joint and not touch a single soul. By this time, usually, they'd be lined up against the bar, and it'd be a dull evening if someone hadn't taken a poke at someone else—although you understand I run a decent place."

"Sure you do," I said. "Sit down and have a drink with us."

"It ain't right that I should," said Joe. "A bartender should never take a drink when he's conducting business. But I feel so low that if you don't mind, I'll take you up on it."

He went back to the bar and got a bottle and a glass and we had quite a few.

The corner he said, had always been a good spot—steady business all the time, with a rush at noon and a good crowd in the evening. But business had started dropping off six weeks before, and now was down to nothing.

"It's the same all over town," he said. "Some places worse than others. This place is one of the worst; I just don't know what's gotten into people."

We said we didn't, either. I fished out some money and left it for the drinks, and we made our escape.

Outside I asked Jo Ann to have dinner with me, but she said it was the night her bridge club met, so I drove her home and went on to my place.

I take a lot of ribbing at the office for living so far out of town, but I like it. I got the cottage cheap, and it's better than living in a couple of cooped-up rooms in a third-rate resident hotel—which would be the best I could afford if I stayed in town.

After I'd fixed up a steak and some fried potatoes for supper, I went down to the dock and rowed out into the lake a ways. I sat there for a while watching the lighted windows winking all around the shore and listening to the sounds you never hear in daytime—the muskrat swimming and the soft chuckling of the ducks and the occasional slap of a jumping fish.

IT WAS a bit chilly and after a little while I rowed back in again, thinking there was a lot to do before winter came. The boat should be caulked and painted; the cottage itself could take a coat of paint, if I could get around to it. There were a couple of storm windows that needed glass replaced, and by rights I should putty all of them. The chimney needed some bricks to replace the ones that had blown off in a windstorm earlier in the year, and the door should have new weather-stripping.

I sat around and read a while and then I went to bed. Just before I went to sleep I thought some about the two old ladies—one of them happy and the other dead.

The next morning I got the community chest story out of the way, first thing; then I got an encyclopedia from the library and did some reading on magnetism. I figured that I should know something about it, before I saw this whiz-bang at the university.

But I needn't have worried so much; this Dr. Thomas turned out to be a regular Joe. We sat around and had quite a talk. He told me about magnetism, and when he found out I lived at the lake he talked about fishing; then we found we knew some of the same people, and it was all right.

Except he didn't have a story.

"There may be one in another year or so," he told me. "When there is, I'll let you in on it."

I'd heard that one before, of course, so I tried to pin him down.

"It's a promise," he said; "you get it first, ahead of anyone."

I let it go at that. You couldn't ask the man to sign a contract on it.

I WAS watching a chance to get away, but I could see he still had more to say. So I stayed on; it's refreshing to find someone who wants to talk to you.

"I think there'll be a story," he said, looking worried, as if he were afraid there mightn't be. "I've worked on it for years. Magnetism is still one of the phenomena we don't know too much about. Once we knew nothing about electricity, and even now we do not entirely understand it; but we found out about it, and when we knew enough about it, we put it to work. We could do the same with magnetism, perhaps—if we only could determine the first fundamentals of it."

He stopped and looked straight at me. "When you were a kid, did you believe in brownies?"

That one threw me and he must have seen it did.

"You remember—the little helpful people. If they liked you, they did all sorts of things for you; and all they expected of you was that you'd leave out a bowl of milk for them."

I told him I'd read the stories, and I supposed that at one time I must have believed in them—although right at the moment I couldn't swear I had.

"If I didn't know better," he said, "I'd think I had brownies in this lab. Someone—or something—shuffled my notes for me. I'd left them on the desk top held down with a paperweight; the next morning they were spread all over, and part of them dumped onto the floor."

"A cleaning woman," I suggested.

He smiled at my suggestion. "I'm the cleaning woman here."

I THOUGHT he had finished and I wondered why all this talk of notes and brownies. I was reaching for my hat when he told me the rest of it.

"There were two sheets of the notes still underneath the paperweight," he said. "One of them had been folded carefully. I was about to pick them up, and put them with the other sheets so I could sort them later, when I happened to read what was on those sheets beneath the paperweight."

He drew a long breath. "They were two sections of my notes that, if left to myself, I probably never would have tied together. Sometimes we have strange blind spots; sometimes we look so closely to a thing that we are blinded to it. And there it was—two sheets laid there by accident. Two sheets, one of them folded to tie up with the other, to show me a possibility I'd never thought of otherwise. I've been working on that possibility ever since. I have hopes it may work out."

"When it does..." I said.

"It is yours," he told me.

I got my hat and left.

And I thought idly of brownies all the way back to the office.

I HAD JUST got back to the office, and settled down for an hour or two of loafing, when old J. H.—our publisher—made one of his irregular pilgrimages of good will out into the newsroom. J. H. is a pompous windbag, without a sincere bone in his body; he knows we know this and we know he knows—but he, and all the rest of us, carry out the comedy of good fellowship to its bitter end.

He stopped beside my desk, clapped me on the shoulder, and said in a voice that boomed throughout the newsroom: "That's a tremendous job you're doing on the community chest, my boy."

Feeling a little sick and silly, I got to my feet and said, "Thank you, J. H. It's nice of you to say so."

Which was what was expected of, me. It was almost ritual.

He grabbed me by the hand, put the other hand on my shoulder, shook my hand vigorously and squeezed my shoulder hard. And I'll be damned if there weren't tears in his eyes as he told me, "You just stick around, Mark, and keep up the work. You won't regret it for a minute. We may not always show it, but we appreciate good work and loyalty and we're always watching what you do out here."

Then he dropped me like a hot potato and went on with his greetings.

I sat down again; the rest of the day was ruined for me. I told myself that if I deserved any commendation I could have hoped it would be for something other than the community chest stories. They were lousy stories; I knew it, and so did the Barnacle and all the rest of them.

No one blamed me for their being lousy—you can't write anything but a lousy story on a community chest drive. But they weren't cheering me.

And I had a sinking feeling that, somehow, old J. H. had found out about the applications I had planted with a half dozen other papers and that this was his gentle way of letting me know he knew—and that I had better watch my step.

CHAPTER THREE

JUST BEFORE noon, Steve Johnson—who handles the medical run along with whatever else the Barnacle can find for him to do—came over to my desk. He had a bunch of clippings in his hand and he was looking worried. "I hate to ask you this, Mark," he said, "but would you help me out?"

"Sure thing, Steve."

"It's an operation. I have to check on it, but I won't have the time, I got to run out to the airport and catch an interview."

He laid the clips down on my desk. "It's all in there."

Then he was off for his interview.

I picked up the clippings and read them through; it was a story that would break your heart.

There was this little fellow, about three years old, who had to have an operation on his heart. It was a piece of surgery that had been done only a time or two before, and then only in big eastern hospitals by famous medical names—and never on one as young as three.

I hated to pick up the phone and call; I was almost sure of the kind of answer I would get.

But I did, and naturally I ran into the kind of trouble you always run into when you try to get some information out of a hospital staff—as if they were shining pure and you were a dirty, little mongrel trying to sneak in. But I finally got hold of someone who told me the boy seemed to be O. K. and that the operation appeared to be successful.

So I called the surgeon who had done the job. I must have caught him in one of his better moments, for he filled me in on some information that fit into the story.

"You are to be congratulated, doctor," I told him and he got a little testy.

"Young man," he told me, "in an operation such as this the surgeon is no more than a single factor. There are so many other factors that no one can take credit."

Then suddenly he sounded tired and scared. "It was a miracle," he said. "But don't you quote me on that," he fairly shouted at me.

"I wouldn't think of it," I told him.

Then I called the hospital again, and talked to the mother of the boy.

IT WAS a good story. We caught the home edition with it, a four-column-head on the left side of page one, and the Barnacle slipped a cog or two and gave me a byline on it.

After lunch I went back to Jo Ann's desk; she was in a tizzy. The Barnacle had thrown a church convention program at her and she was in the midst of writing an advance story, listing all the speakers and committee members and special panels and events. It's the deadliest kind of a story you can be told to write; it's worse, even, than the community chest.

I listened to her being bitter for quite a while, then I asked her if she figured she'd have any strength left when the day was over.

"I'm all pooped out," she said.

"Reason I asked," I told her, "is that I want to take the boat out of the water and I need some one to help me."

"Mark," she said, "if you expect me to go out there and horse a boat around..."

"You wouldn't have to lift," I told her. "Maybe just tug a little. We'll use a block and tackle to lift it on the blocks so that later I can paint it. All I need is someone to steady it while I haul it up."

She still wasn't sold on it, so I laid out some bait.

"We could stop downtown and pick up a couple of lobsters." I told her. "You are good at lobsters. I could make some of my Roquefort dressing, and we could have a…"

"But without the garlic," she said. So I promised to forego the garlic and she agreed to come.

SOMEHOW or other, we never did get that boat out of the water; there were so many other things to do.

After dinner we built a fire in the fireplace and sat in front of it. She put her head on my shoulder and we were comfortable and cozy. "Let's play pretend," she said. "Let's pretend you have that job you want. Let's say it is in London, and this is a lodge in the English fens…"

"A fen," I said, "is a hell of a place to have a lodge."

"You always spoil things," she complained. "Let's start over again. Let's pretend you have that job you want…"

And she stuck to her fens.

Driving back to the lake after taking her home, I wondered if I'd ever get that job. Right at the moment it didn't look so rosy. Not that I couldn't have handled it, for I knew I could. I had racks of books on world affairs, and I kept close track of what was going on. I had a good command of French, a working knowledge of German, and off and on I was struggling with Spanish. It was something I'd wanted all my life—to feel that I was a part of that fabulous newspaper fraternity that kept check around the world.

I OVERSLEPT, and was late to work in the morning. The Barnacle took a sour view of it. "Why did you bother to come in at all?" he growled at me. "Why do you ever bother to come in? Last two days I sent you out on two assignments, and where are the stories?"

"There weren't any stories," I told him, trying to keep my temper. "They were just some more pipe dreams you dug up."

"Someday," he said, "when you get to be a real reporter, you'll dig up stories for yourself. That's what's the matter with this staff," he said in a sudden burst of anger. "That's what's wrong with you. No initiative; sit around and wait; wait until I dig up something I can send you out on. No one ever surprises me and brings in a story I haven't sent them out on."

He pegged me with his eyes. "Why don't you just once surprise me?"

"I'll surprise you, buster," I said and walked over to my desk.

I sat there thinking. I thought about old Mrs. Clayborne, who had been dying hard—and then suddenly had died easy. I remembered what the gardener had told me, and the footprint I had found underneath the window. I thought of that other old lady who had been a hundred years old, and how all her old, dead friends had come visiting. And about the physicist who had brownies in his lab. And about the boy and his successful operation.

And I got an idea.

I went to the files and went through them three weeks back, page by page. I took a lot of notes and got a little scared, but told myself it was nothing but coincidence.

Then I sat down at my typewriter and made half a dozen false starts, but finally I had it.

The brownies have come back again, I wrote.

You know, those little people who do all sorts of good deeds for you, and expect nothing in return except that you set out a bowl of milk for them.

At the time I didn't realize that I was using almost the exact words the physicist had said.

I DIDN'T write about Mrs. Clayborne, or the old lady with her visitors, or the physicist, or the little boy who had the operation; those weren't things you could write about with your tongue in cheek, and that's the way I wrote it.

But I did write about the little two and three paragraph items I had found tucked away in the issues I had gone through—the good luck stories; the little happy stories of no consequence, except for the ones they had happened to—about people finding things they'd lost months or years ago, about stray dogs coming home, and kids winning essay contests, and neighbor helping neighbor. All the kindly little news stories that we'd thrown in just to fill up awkward holes.

There were a lot of them—a lot more, it seemed to me, than you could normally expect to find. *All these things happened in our town in the last three weeks,* I wrote at the end of it.

And I added one last line: *Have you put out that bowl of milk?*

After it was finished, I sat there for a while, debating whether I should hand it in. And thinking it over, I decided that the Barnacle had it coming to him, after the way he'd shot off his mouth.

So I threw it into the basket on the city desk and went back to write the community chest story.

The Barnacle never said a thing to me and I didn't say a thing to him; you could have knocked my eyes off with a stick when the kid brought the papers up from the pressroom, and there was my brownie story spread across the top of page one in an eight-column feature strip.

No one mentioned it to me except Jo Ann, who came along and patted me on the head and said she was proud of me—although God knows why she should have been.

Then the Barnacle sent me out on another one of his wild-goose chases concerning someone who was supposed to be building a homemade atomic pile in his back yard. It turned out that this fellow is an old geezer who, at one time, had built a perpetual motion machine that didn't work. Once I found that out, I was so disgusted that I didn't even go back to the office, but went straight home instead.

I RIGGED up a block and tackle, had some trouble what with no one to help me, but I finally got the boat up on the blocks. Then I drove to a little village at the end of the lake and bought paint for not only the boat, but the cottage as well. I felt pretty good about making such a fine start on all the work I should do that fall.

The next morning when I got to the office, I found the place in an uproar. The switchboard had been clogged all night and it still looked like a Christmas tree. One of the operators had passed out, and they were trying to bring her to.

The Barnacle had a wild gleam in his eye, and his necktie was all-askew. When he saw me, he took me firmly by the arm and led me to my desk and sat me down. "Now, damn you, get to work!" he yelled and he dumped a bale of notes down in front of me.

"What's going on?" I asked.

"It' s that brownie deal of yours," he yelled. "Thousands of people are calling in. All of them have brownies; they've been helped by brownies; some of them have even seen brownies."

"What about the milk?" I asked.

"Milk? What milk?"

"Why, the milk they should set out for them."

"How do I know," he said. "Why don't you call up some of the milk companies and find out."

THAT IS just what I did and, so help me Hannah, the milk companies were slowly going crazy. Every driver had come racing back to get extra milk, because most of their customers were ordering an extra quart or so. They were lined up for blocks outside the stations waiting for new loads and the milk supply was running low.

There weren't any of us in the newsroom that morning who did anything but write brownie copy. We filled the paper with it—all sorts of stories about how the brownies had been helping people. Except, of course, they hadn't known it was brownies helping them until they read my story. They'd just thought that it was good luck.

When the first edition was in, we sat back and sort of caught our breath—although the calls still were coming in--and I swear my typewriter still was hot from the copy I'd turned out.

The papers came up, and each of us took our copy and started to go through it, when we heard a roar from J. H.'s office. A second later, J. H. came out himself, waving a paper in his fist, his face three shades redder than a brand-new fire truck.

He practically galloped to the city desk and he flung the paper down in front of the Barnacle and hit it with his fist. "What do you mean?" he shouted. "Explain yourself. Making us ridiculous!"

"But, J. H. I thought it was a good gag and…"

"*Brownies*," J. H. snorted.

"We got all those calls," said Barnacle Bill. "They still are coming in. And…"

"That's enough," J. H. thundered. "You're fired!"

He swung around from the city desk and looked straight at me. "You're the one who started it," he said. "You're fired, too."

I got up from my chair and moved over to the city desk. "We'll be back a little later," I told J. H., "to collect our severance pay."

He flinched a little at that, but he didn't back up any.

The Barnacle picked up an ashtray off his desk and let it fall. It hit the floor and broke. He dusted off his hands. "Come on, Mark," he said. "I'll buy you a drink."

CHAPTER FOUR

WE WENT over to the corner. Joe brought us a bottle and a couple of glasses, and we settled down to business.

Pretty soon some of the other boys started dropping in. They'd have a drink or two with us and then go back to work. It was their way of showing us they were sorry the way things had turned out. They didn't say anything, but they kept dropping in. There never was a time during the entire afternoon when there wasn't some one drinking with us. The Barnacle and I took on quite a load.

We talked over this brownie business, and at first we were a little skeptical about it, laying the situation more or less to public gullibility. But the more we thought about it, and the more we drank, the more we began to believe there might be really brownies. For one thing, good luck just doesn't come in hunks the way it appeared to have come to this town of ours in the last few weeks. Good luck is apt to scatter itself around a bit—and while it may run in streaks, it's usually pretty thin. But here it seemed that hundreds—if not thousands—of persons had been visited by good luck.

BY THE middle of the afternoon, we were fairly well agreed there might be something to this brownie business. Then of course, we tried to figure out who the brownies were, and why they were helping people.

"You know what I think," said the Barnacle. "I think they're aliens. People from the stars. Maybe they're the ones who have been flying all these saucers."

"But why would aliens want to help us?" I objected. "Sure, they'd want to watch us and find out all they could; and after a while, they might try to make contact with us. They might even be willing to help us—but if they were they'd want to help us as a race, but as individuals."

"Maybe" the Barnacle suggested, "they're just busybodies. There are humans like that. Psychopathic do-gooders, always sticking in their noses, never letting well enough alone."

"I don't think so," I argued back at him. "If they are trying to help us, I'd guess it's a religion with them. Like the old friars who wandered all over Europe in the early days. Like the Good Samaritan. Like the Salvation Army."

But he wouldn't have it that way. "They're busybodies," he insisted. "Maybe they come from a surplus economy, a planet where all the work is gone by machines and there is more than enough of everything for everyone. Maybe there isn't anything left for anyone to do—and you know yourself that a man has to have something to keep him occupied, something to do so he can think that he is important."

Then along about five o'clock Jo Ann came in. It had been her day off and she hadn't known what had happened until someone from the office phoned her. So she'd come right over.

She was plenty sore at me, and she wouldn't listen to me when I tried to explain that at a time like this a man had to have a drink or two. She got me out of there and out back to my car and drove me to her place. She fed me black coffee and finally gave me something to eat and along about eight o'clock or so she figured I'd sobered up enough to try driving home.

I TOOK it easy and I made it, but I had an awful head and I remembered that I didn't have a job. Worst of all, I was probably tagged for life as the man who had dreamed up the brownie hoax. There was no doubt that the wire services had picked up the story, and that it had made front page in most of the papers coast to coast. No doubt, the radio and television commentators were doing a lot of chuckling at it.

My cottage stands up on a sharp little rise above the lake, a sort of hog's back between the lake and road, and there's no road up to it. I had to leave my car alongside the road at the foot of the rise, and walk up to the place.

I walked along, my head bent a little so I could see the path in the moonlight and I was almost to the cottage before I heard a sound that made me raise my head.

And there they were.

They had rigged up a scaffold and there were four of them on it, painting the cottage madly. Three of them were up on the roof replacing the bricks that had been knocked out of the chimney. They had storm windows scattered all over the place and were furiously applying putty to them. And you could scarcely see the boat, there were so many of them slapping paint on it.

I stood there staring at them, with my jaw hanging on my breastbone, when I heard a sudden swish and stepped quickly to one side. About a dozen of them rushed by, reeling out the hose, running down the hill with it. Almost in a shorter time than it takes to tell it, they were washing the car.

They didn't seem to notice me. Maybe it was because they were so busy they didn't have the time to—or it might have been just that it wasn't proper etiquette to take notice of someone when they were helping him.

THEY LOOKED a lot like the brownies that you see pictured in the children's books, but there were differences. They wore pointed caps, all right, but when I got close to one of them who was busy puttying, I could see that it was no cap at all. His head ran up to a point, and, that the tassel on the top of it was no tassel of a cap, but a tuft of hair or feathers—I couldn't make out which. They wore coats with big fancy buttons on them, but I got the impression—I don't know how—that they weren't buttons, but something else entirely. And instead of the big sloppy clown-type shoes they're usually shown as wearing, they had nothing on their feet.

They worked hard and fast; they didn't waste a minute. They didn't walk, but ran. And there were so many of them.

Suddenly they were finished. The boat was painted, and so was the cottage. The puttied, painted storm windows were leaned against the trees. The hose was dragged up the hill and neatly coiled again.

I saw that they were finishing and I tried to call them all together so that I could thank them, but they paid no attention to me. And when they were finished, they were gone. I was left standing, all alone—with the newly painted cottage shining in the moonlight and the smell of paint heavy in the air.

I suppose I wasn't exactly sober, despite the night air and all the coffee Jo Ann had poured into me. If I had been cold, stone sober I might have done it better; I might have thought of something. As it was, I'm afraid I bungled it.

I staggered into the house, and the outside door seemed a little hard to shut. When I looked for the reason, I saw it had been weather-stripped.

With the lights on, I looked around—and in all the time I'd been there the place had never been so neat. There wasn't a speck of dust on anything and all the metal shone. All the pots and pans were neatly stacked in place—all the clothing I had left strewn around had been put away; all the books were lined straight within the shelves, and the magazines were where they should be instead of just thrown anywhere.

I MANAGED to get into bed, and I tried to think about it; but someone came along with a heavy mallet and hit me on the head and that was the last I knew until I was awakened by a terrible racket.

I got to it as fast as I could.

"What is it now?" I snarled, which is no way to answer a phone, but was the way I felt.

It was J. H. "What's the matter with you?" he yelled. "Why aren't you at the office? What do you mean by…"

"Just a minute, J. H. Don't you remember? You canned me yesterday."

"Now, Mark," he said, "you wouldn't hold that against me, would you? We were all excited…"

"*I* wasn't excited," I told him.

"Look," he said. "I need you. There's someone here to see you."

"All right," I said and hung up.

I DIDN'T hurry any; I took my time. If J. H. needed me, if there was someone there to see me, both of them could wait. I turned on the coffee maker and took a shower; after the shower and coffee, I felt almost human.

I was crossing the yard, heading for the path down to the car when I saw something that stopped me like a shot.

There were tracks in the dust, tracks all over the place—exactly the kind of tracks I'd seen in the flower bed underneath the window at the Clayborne estate. I squatted down and looked closely at them to make sure there was no mistake and there couldn't be. They were the self-same tracks.

They were brownie tracks!

I stayed there for a long time, squatting beside the tracks and thinking that now it was all believable because there was no longer any room for disbelief.

The nurse had been right; there had been something in the room that night Mrs. Clayborne died. It was a mercy, the old gardener had said, his thoughts and speech all fuzzed with the weariness and the basic simplicity of the very old. An act of mercy, a good deed, for the old lady had been dying hard, no hope for her.

And if there were good deeds in death, there were as well in life. In an operation such as this, the surgeon had told me, there are so many factors that no one can take the credit. *It was a miracle*, he'd said, *but don't you quote me on it.*

And someone—no cleaning woman, but someone or something else—had messed up the notes of the physicist and in the messing of them had put together two pages out of several hundred—two pages that tied together and made sense.

Coincidence? I asked myself. Coincidence that a woman died and that a boy lived, and that a researcher got a clue he'd otherwise have missed? No, not coincidence when there was a track beneath a window and papers scattered from beneath paperweight.

And—I'd almost forgotten—Jo Ann's old lady who sat rocking happily because all her old dead friends had come to visit her. There were even times when senility might become a very kindness.

I straightened up and went down to the car. As, I drove into town I kept thinking about the magic touch of kindness from the stars or if, perhaps, there might be upon this earth, co-existent with the human race, another race that had a different outlook and a different way of life. A race, perhaps, that had tried time and time again to ally itself with the humans and each time had been rejected and driven into hiding—sometimes by ignorance and superstition and again by a too-brittle knowledge of what was impossible. A race, perhaps, that might be trying once again.

CHAPTER FIVE

J. H. WAS waiting for me, looking, exactly like a cat sitting serenely inside a birdcage…with feathers on his whiskers. With him was a high brass flyboy, who had a rainbow of decorations spread across his jacket and eagles on his shoulders. They shone so bright and earnestly that they almost sparkled.

"Mark, this is Colonel Duncan," said J. H. "He'd like to have a word with you."

The two of us shook hands and the colonel was more affable than one would have expected him to be. Then J. H. left us in his office and shut the door behind him. The two of us sat down and each of us sort of measured up the other. I don't know how the colonel felt, but I was ready to admit I was uncomfortable. I wondered what I might have done and what the penalty might be.

"I wonder, Lathrop," said the colonel, "if you'd mind telling me exactly how it happened? How you found out about the brownies?"

"I didn't find out about them, Colonel; it was just a gag."

I TOLD him about the Barnacle shooting off his mouth about no one on the staff ever showing any initiative, and how I'd dreamed up the brownie story to get even with him. And how the Barnacle had got even with me by running it.

But that didn't satisfy the colonel. "There must be more to it than that," he said.

I could see that he'd keep at me until I'd told it anyhow; and while he hadn't said a word about it, I kept seeing images of the Pentagon, and the chiefs of staff, and Project Saucer—or whatever they might call it now—and the FBI, and a lot of other unpleasant things just over his left shoulder.

So I came clean with him. I told him all of it and a lot of it, I granted, sounded downright silly.

But he didn't seem to think that it was silly. "And what do you think about all this?"

"I don't know," I told him. "They might come from outer space, or…"

He nodded quietly. "We've known for some time now, that there have been landings. This is the first time they've ever deliberately called attention to themselves."

"What do they want, Colonel? What are they aiming at?"

"I wish I knew."

Then he said very quietly. "Of course, if you should write anything about this, I simply shall deny it. That will leave you in a most peculiar position at the best."

I don't know how much more he might have told me—maybe quite a bit. But right then the phone rang. I picked it up and answered; it was for the colonel.

He said "yes," and listened. He didn't say another word. He got a little white around the gills, then he hung up the phone.

HE SAT there, looking sick.

"What's the matter, Colonel?"

"That was the field," he told me. "It happened just a while ago. They came out of nowhere and swarmed all over the plane—polished it and cleaned it and made it spic-and-span, both inside and out. The men couldn't do a thing about it. They just had to stand and watch."

I grinned. "There's nothing bad about that, Colonel. They were just being good to you."

"You don't know the half of it," he said. "When they got it all prettied up, they painted a brownie on the nose."

That's just about all there's to it so far as the brownies are concerned. The job they did on the colonel's plane was, actually, the sole public appearance that they made. But it was enough to serve their purpose if publicity was what they wanted—a sort of visual clincher, as it were. One of our photographers—a loopy character by the name of Charles, who never was where you wanted him when you wanted him, but nevertheless seemed to be exactly on the spot when the unusual or disaster struck—was out at the airport that morning. He wasn't supposed to be there; he was supposed to be covering a fire, which turned out luckily to be no more than a minor blaze. How he managed to wind up at the airport even he, himself, never was able to explain. But he was there and he got the pictures of the brownies polishing up the plane—not only one or two pictures, but a couple dozen of them, all the plates he had. Another thing—he got the pictures with a telescopic lens. He'd put it in his bag that morning by mistake; he'd never carried it before. After that one time he never was without it again and, to my knowledge, never had another occasion where he had to use it.

THOSE pictures were a bunch of lulus. We used the best of them on page one—a solid page of them—and ran two more pages of the rest inside. The AP got hold of them, transmitted them, and a number of other member papers used them before someone at the Pentagon heard about it and promptly blew his stack. But no matter what the Pentagon might say, the pictures had been run and whatever harm—*or good*—they might have done could not be recalled.

I suppose that if the colonel had known about them, he'd have warned us not to use them and might have confiscated them. But no one knew the pictures had been taken until the colonel was out of town, and probably back in Washington. Charlie got waylaid somehow—at a beer joint most likely—and didn't get back to the office until the middle of the afternoon.

When he heard about it, J. H. paced up and down and tore his hair and threatened to fire Charlie; but some of the rest of us got him calmed down and back into his office. We caught the pictures in our final street edition, picked the pages up for the early run's next day, and the circulation boys were pop-eyed for days at the way those papers sold.

The next day, after the worst of the excitement had subsided, the Barnacle and I went down to the corner to have ourselves a couple. I had never cared too much for the Barnacle before, but the fact that we'd been fired together established a sort of bond between us; and he didn't seem to be such a bad sort, after all.

JOE WAS as sad as ever. "It's them brownies," he old us, and he described them in a manner no one should ever use when talking of a brownie. "They've gone and made everyone so happy they don't need to drink no more."

"Both you and me, Joe," said the Barnacle, "they ain't done nothing for me, either."

"You got your job back," I told him.

"Mark," he said, solemnly, pouring out another, "I'm not so sure if that is good or not."

It might have developed into a grade-A crying session if Lightning, our most up-and-coming copy boy, had not come shuffling in at that very moment.

"Mr. Lathrop," he said, "there's a phone call for you."

"Well, that's just fine."

"But it's from New York," said the kid.

That did it. It's the first time in my life I ever left a place so fast that I forgot my drink.

The call was from one of the papers to which I had applied, and the man at the New York end told me there was a job opening in the London staff and that he'd like to talk with me about it. In itself, it probably wasn't any better than the job I had, he said, but it would give me a chance to break in on the kind of work I wanted.

When could I come in? he asked, and I said tomorrow morning.

I hung up and sat back and the world all at once looked rosy. I knew right then and there those brownies still were working for me.

I HAD A lot of time to think on the plane trip to New York; and while I spent some of it thinking about the new job and London, I spent a lot of it thinking about the brownies, too.

They'd come to Earth before, that much at least was clear. And the world had not been ready for them. It had muffled them in a fog of folklore and superstition, and had lacked the capacity to use what they had offered it. Now they tried again. This time we must not fail them, for there might not be a third time.

Perhaps one of the reasons they had failed before—although not the only reason—had been the lack of a media of mass communications. The story of them, and of their deeds and doings, had gone by word of mouth and had been distorted in the telling. The fantasy of the age attached itself to the story of the brownies until they became no more than a magic little people who were very droll, and one occasion helpful, but in the same category as the ogre, or the dragon, and others of their ilk.

Today it had been different. Today there was a better chance the brownies would be objectively reported. And while the entire story could not be told immediately, the people still could guess.

And that was important—the publicity they got. People must know they were back again, and must believe in them and trust them.

And why, I wondered, had one medium-sized city in the midwest of America been chosen as the place where they would make known their presence and demonstrate their worth? I puzzled a lot about that one, but I never did get it figured out, not even to this day.

JO ANN WAS waiting for me at the airport when I came back from New York with the job tucked in my pocket. I was looking for her when I came down the ramp, and I saw that she'd got past the gate and was running toward the plane. I raced out to meet her and I scooped her up and kissed her and some damn fool popped a flash bulb at us. I wanted to mop up on him, but Jo Ann wouldn't let me.

It was early evening and you could see some stars shining in the sky, despite the blinding floodlights; from way up, you could hear another plane that had just taken off; and up at the far end of the field, another one was warming up. There were the buildings and the lights and the people and the great machines and it seemed, for a long moment, like a tableau built to represent the strength and swiftness, the competence and assurance of this world of ours.

Jo Ann must have felt it, too, for she said suddenly: "It's nice, Mark. I wonder if they'll change it."

I knew who she meant without even asking.

"I think I know what they are," I told her. "I think I got it figured out. You know that community chest drive that's going on right now. Well, that's what they are doing, too—a sort of galactic chest. Except that they aren't spending money on the poor and needy; their kind of charity is a different sort. Instead of spending money on us, they're spending love and kindness, neighborliness and brotherhood. And I guess that it's all right. I wouldn't wonder but that, of all the people in the universe, we are the ones who need it most. They didn't come to solve all our problems for us—just to help clear away some of the little problems that somehow keep us from turning our full power on the important jobs, or keep us from looking at them in the right way."

THAT WAS more years ago than I like to think about, but I still can remember just as if it were yesterday.

Something happened yesterday that brought it all to mind again.

I happened to be in Downing Street, not too far from No. 10, when I saw a little fellow I first took to be some sort of dwarf. When I turned to look at him, I saw that he was watching me; he raised one hand in an emphatic gesture, with the thumb and first finger made into a circle—the good, solid American signal that everything's okay.

Then he disappeared. He probably ducked into an alley, although I can't say for a fact that I actually saw him go.

But he was right. Everything's okay.

The world is bright, and the cold war is all but over. We may be entering upon the first true peace the human race has ever known.

Jo Ann is packing, and crying as she packs, because she has to leave so many things behind. But the kids are goggle-eyed about the great adventure just ahead. Tomorrow morning we leave for Peking, where I'll be the first accredited American correspondent for almost thirty years.

And I can't help but wonder if, perhaps, somewhere in that ancient city—perhaps in a crowded, dirty street; perhaps along the imperial highway; maybe some day out in the country beside the Great Wall, built so fearsomely so many years ago—I may not see another little man.

THE END

Secret of the Burning Finger

By JOHN W. JAKES

Nobody could stand between Geller and that buried silver—and live. But it seems there are forces stronger than any man...

GELLER kept his hands tightly clenched upon the wheel. The dash lights of the truck's sealed pressurized cab made patches of brilliance on his long taciturn face. Beyond the windows, the rocky fields of the moon rolled by under the star-hung night. The truck wheels, clinging to the road with their sealed-in gravity plates, threw into the void veils of white pumice like ghostly fingers.

To the right of the road rose the Leibnitz Mountains, towering piles of twisting rock thirty thousand feet high. Geller smiled thinly, glancing at them.

They held their secret so quietly, locked in the hardness. Other men had tried to wrest the treasure from them, and failed. But Geller felt he would succeed, and with success would come the easy life among the wealthy people of the system that, as a freight-handler at the Luna City docks, or a waiter on the asteroid yachts, he had always longed for.

The road curved abruptly, and crawled at an angle toward a high hill. Geller tensed expectantly and shoved the accelerator to the floor.

The truck careened over the brink of the hill.

At the foot of the mountains sat a hemisphere of whiteness, housing the small frontier town of New Taos. And beyond that, where the mountains rose, stood the Burning Finger, washed in a harsh silver glow. In that pointing bit of rock, some ten thousand feet high, lay all of Geller's hopes.

There was a dead man in a tiny hotel back at Port-of-the-Moon, an old lunar pioneer who had spent his younger days, among other places, in the Leibnitz range. The key to the Burning Finger had been his, and Geller had stuck a knife in his belly and taken it from him.

As he drove on, the roadway leveled out. The glassteel shell that surrounded New Taos and held its atmosphere, bulged from the pumice plain like a great beetle against the shining mountains and the icy dark.

Geller felt sweat under his jacket. He patted his shirt, making sure he had the credentials, then applied the brake as the truck crunched to a halt before the transparent wall.

He flashed his lights, and a section of the wall moved upward. He drove forward a few feet into the airlock. As he opened the cab door, he heard the rush of air entering the chamber. A wall port opened and one of the Mexican guards walked over, peering at him with alert brown eyes.

"Bowman," the man in the truck said, handing down the identity card.

"You are a trader, *senor?*" the guard inquired.

"That's right." He held the wheel tightly, knowing his hands would tremble if he did not.

"There is no picture of you on this card, *Senor* Bowman. All identity cards require…"

Well, he had known all along that it might trip him up. He had changed cards with a barkeep in Luna City who had a freedom of movement visa. But the barkeep hadn't been willing to let Geller keep the picture from his own card, and the picture of the man called Bowman was useless to him.

"I lost it," Geller bluffed. "I was in a fight at Iowatown, and I lost it."

"Por favor, senor," the guard began, "you must produce—"

"For God's sake," Geller said sharply. "Do you think I'd be out here if it wasn't for my business?" He tried to appear disgusted. "The days of criminals escaping on the moon are pretty well over. I'll be damned if I'll go all the way back just because I haven't got a picture."

The guard hesitated, then tried to smile as he observed Geller carefully. *"Si senor.* Of course you cannot go back." He pressed a lever and the inner lock door rose.

"Pass," he said, gesturing broadly.

A tight quirk of humor played on Geller's mouth as he yanked the shift and stepped on the accelerator. The truck rolled into the main street of New Taos.

And the first barrier was behind him.

IT WAS a drowsy little place, layed out wheel-like about a central plaza. At the far side of the town rose the hydroponic bean factory, its only industry. The townspeople, a mixture of Mexican, Indian and American bloods, lived life slowly in the dusty streets. The buildings for the most part were of clay. And despite the silver bulk of a small-rocked port office, the town managed to maintain an air of Southwestern America, from which most of its inhabitants had migrated.

Geller drove slowly, avoiding fat roosters waddling in the road. Two boys in white shirts and trousers wrestled in an alley mouth. Somewhere a guitar whispered, and a voice was lifted in the haunting *Senora del Sol.*

The air was artificially pungent and soft dusky light sifted down from the roof of the hemisphere high above. Geller parked in a lot beside a low building marked *New Taos Cantina.*

He climbed down, making sure that the gun at his hip was full, and walked to the bar entrance. There, he turned and looked beyond the glassteel wall of the city.

The Burning Finger reared its impregnable slender brilliance aloft, against the background of the range. The shaft of stone seemed haughty.

"I've got you," Geller murmured, and pushed through the Cantina door.

A few men were at the bar, drinking and speaking softly. Soames sat off in a corner, rubbing his dirty yellow mustache and blinking his eyes from behind folds of pink fat. He glanced up, saw Geller, then stared down at the table again.

"Terran whisky," Geller said to the barkeep. "Give me the bottle."

He threw down a solar, took the bottle and walked over to Soames. He sat down with his back to the bar and lit a cigarette.

"Took you long enough," Soames grumbled.

"Try driving that road sometime."

Soames shrugged, steering clear of an argument in exactly the same way he avoided work. "Any trouble?"

"Not much. I couldn't keep my picture when I traded identity cards. But the guard at the lock was willing enough to be talked down." He poured two drinks. Soames gulped his immediately.

"Got the fork?" he asked. The whisky made sucking rivers through his mustache.

"In the truck . And don't talk so goddamned loud."

Soames blinked. "All right. All right, only I want to get this over with. Maybe what the old man at Port-of-the-Moon said wasn't right. Maybe there isn't anything in the Burning Finger at all."

"But he had some of the silver," Geller replied, striking his fist on the table for emphasis. "He used the fork to open it a year ago, and he got some of the silver, but he didn't have any way of transporting it. He got pumice-cough and had to lay up for a while."

"Maybe it wasn't silver," Soames insisted. "Maybe—"

"Listen," Geller growled. "Twenty-eight years ago Jamie Lachlin and some of the others from Moonhole hijacked the *Megathon* with ten thousand solars in silver ingots for the Luna City government buildings. The old man was with Lachlin, and he said they buried it in a crypt in the Burning Finger, and went into hiding. There wasn't any town here then, and all the men except the oldster got killed off by the law. The treasure is a legend on Luna. Others have tried to dig out the stuff, and failed. Now we've got it for certain.

"Things like this only happen once in a man's span of years. We were sitting in the hotel when the old guy walks in drunk and starts talking. When you get a chance like that, you *make* it payoff!"

"Are you sure no one found the body when you got the fork?" Soames asked quickly. "If anyone…"

"I sent you out here to arrange for the rocket, not to worry about me. Did you fix things?"

"Yes. Yes, I did." Soames watched the table morosely. "Class F Jumper, gyro piloted to Luna City. Two hundred solars. All we had. It's ready right now, down at the port."

Geller laughed. "Don't worry. By tomorrow night, we'll have a fortune. Once we've loaded it in the ship, I can tinker with the gyro and we can fly our own course. Right out to Venus."

"When do we get started?" asked Soames.

"There's no sense in waiting. We might as well—"

Geller's fingers constricted on the whisky glass. He kept his eyes narrowed, not looking around. The muted talking of men at the bar had suddenly ceased. And the faraway guitar was silent.

Soames had his eyes wide open. Sweat made small beads on his mustache.

"Senor," said a voice behind Geller.

Slowly, he stood up and turned around.

THERE WERE two of them. The guard from the air lock and a Terran officer from the rocket port. The Earthman's face was square like a stone chunk. His eyes searched Geller's, and he kept his blue automatic leveled at the other man's chest.

"Is your name Geller?" the Earthman said.

"No. Bowman. P hillip Bowman."

"We have a description of you," the officer said quietly, "from Control Police at Port-of-the-Moon. You killed an old man in a hotel there. A clerk reported your description when he saw you coming out of the room. We got it on the standard viz release."

"You're mistaken," Geller said. The Mexican was watching him with fearful eyes. The others along the bar were silent interested spectators. Soames was whispering something under his breath.

"No, I'm not mistaken. Raffertez here reported to me that you came into town without an identity picture. We always check such matters. He gave me a description. Both descriptions match."

"I told you," Soames mumbled thickly. "I told you to be careful..."

"Keep quiet," Geller snapped.

"What are you going to do with us?"

"Take you to the rocket port and ship you back on the mail shuttle."

"Let me finish my drink." He moved his hand toward the glass, and grabbed for his gun. The officer shot and Geller ducked, swinging his weapon into line. It blasted once, loudly. The rocket officer sagged at the knees and collapsed in a twisted heap.

Geller swung the gun on the rest of the men. "Stay right where you are, Soames, get out to the truck and get the box from the dash compartment."

Soames moved his fat bulk rapidly, uttering faint bleats of terror. Geller backed through the door.

"I've got the box," Soames wheezed behind him.

"Hold on to it. It's the fork."

He slammed the doors. "Run," he said quickly, "to the rocket port."

They dashed down the peaceful street. A dark-haired woman jumped out of their way and began to curse in Spanish.

"We can't get away," Soames was puffing. "We can't get away."

"We've come this far," Geller yelled, turning to see the men just beginning to come from the Cantina. "We're going to get the silver!"

They raced across the plaza and down another street. At the end stood the metal bulk of the rocket station. A guard saw them running and lifted his rifle tentatively.

Geller fired twice, and the guard dropped. Heads stuck themselves from windows, then pulled back hastily. The bean factory whistle began to scream.

Out of breath, the two staggered into the office. Two secretaries retreated against one wall. By that time, Soames and Geller were in the hangar.

A bright red Class F Jumper lay in one angled rack. Her sides were caked with rust, and the inside of the stern tube was sticky with sediment.

"Inside," Geller ordered. A Mexican mechanic peered from within the main tube on the nearby mail rocket. Geller shot at him and he ducked back.

Soames heaved himself up the ladder and through the companionway. Geller followed, slamming the port and locking it.

He swung into the shock seat in the control room, Soames in the other. His hands flicked over the banks of switches, and threw home a toggle.

The jets hummed with a troubled, coughing roar.

Geller touched another stud and a red light outside the cabin winked. The doors of the launching rack yawned and the tractor platform moved the ship into the airlock. Something clanged behind them, an indicator showed that the air had been removed, and the outer doors opened.

The black sky soared over them, alight with the witch fire gleams of the distant stars.

"We've got to get off Luna," Soames said. "No time to lose."

"There's a job to do first," Geller said.

He smashed his palm on the stud marked *Accelerate.*

THE ROCKET shuddered and was flung out through the wall of the city. The jets took hold, and the dusty landscape dropped away below them, white and shining.

Geller made rapid adjustments on the gyro control. He unwound the tape, cut tiny alternate notches with his fingernails, and re-fed it hastily into the coordinator. His face was drawn tight.

"Venus," Soames said, reaching for the tape with sweaty pink hands. "Venus. Set the course for Venus."

"The tape is set for pilot control," Geller told him, closing the lid of the gyro case with a snap. He laid his hands on the tube control keys. "We're heading for the silver."

Soames babbled helplessly about running away. Geller let his fingers roam over the firing keys, feeling in them the end to his existence of grubbing for a livelihood in the towns and the calcium camps. His fingers went white as he depressed certain keys.

The coughing thunder of the jets drowned out Soames. The ship groaned, swinging ponderously. The landscape tilted and slid beneath them.

"I know I wanted the silver like you did," Soames breathed, clawing at Geller's shoulder, "but I'd rather stay alive. They're probably calling Luna City right now. A Control Police ship will be on the way any time now! Let's get out...for Christ's sake, Geller...let's get out..."

His voice was sandpaper, his face pale and blotchy like spoiled meat.

Added acceleration rocked the ship.

And Geller chuckled quietly.

The Leibnitz Mountains made a solid wall of white in front of the ship. And out of the mountains rose the decaying pinnacle of the Burning Finger.

Soames retched helplessly in the shock chair as Geller maneuvered the ship close to the top of the stone prominence.

At last he jockeyed into the proper position and shut off the jets. Pressure beams, darting down to the surface far below, held them aloft.

Geller reached for the box he had salvaged from the truck. He slipped into a pressure suit and took the helmet from the adjoining locker.

"I'm not going," Soames said. "I don't want it that much."

Geller lifted his gun in one gloved hand. "You're going."

Soames swallowed and reached for a suit. His eyes were smoking madhouses where fear began to twist the brain into strange patterns.

They clanked to the lock, waited for the air to vanish, and stepped outside into a world of blinding whiteness.

The two men stood on the Burning Finger. It was a square column of rock with a wide plateau-like top. This upper surface was tilted at nearly a seventy-five degree angle, and the ship was anchored at one of the lower corners.

Up the long slope of whiteness, there was a square outcropping.

"That's it," Geller murmured tinnily through the headphones. "That's where the silver is."

Soames looked about and clutched at him. A retching sound rattled through the phone.

The drop was ten thousand feet—straight down.

"Get back in the ship," Soames muttered incoherently. "In the ship…"

He started toward the rocket. Geller struck his arm with the gun and dragged him a few feet up the slope.

"Walk ahead of me, Soames. Walk ahead of me or I'll kill you."

SOAMES staggered up the steep slope, chattering crazily in the phone.

They toiled upward, tiny figures against a contrasting background of glaring white mountains and distant black sky.

Soames tripped on a rock. The boulder went careening down the hill, driven out into the airless void beyond the cliff where it swung downward in a long drifting arc. It vanished beyond the bubble of New Taos, still curving toward the ground.

Soames watched the spectacle, fascinated. "I'm not going to do it, Geller. I don't want the silver."

The other man struck him again and they continued their march upward.

They reached the square outcropping and halted. Geller moved a safe distance from Soames and stuck the gun in his belt. With fumbling gloved hands, he opened the black case and pulled out a large tuning fork.

This was the thing he had gotten from the old man, who had worked to make it for twenty long years. A simple tuning fork, but adjusted to give out a special set of vibrations. The old man had remembered the secret of opening the crypt from his earlier days, and labored to recast another key to the treasure.

Soames watched from inside his helmet like a man caged. His eyes blinked with monotonous regularity in the white glare.

Geller waited, looking at the fork. So much was wrapped up in that small instrument. He almost did not have the courage to use it.

But there was another strength pouring through him. The strength of security, and a rich easy life. That was the prime driving force, overcoming all others.

He struck the fork on his boot and held it against the rock. He could feel it transmitting forced vibration.

For a minute, nothing happened.

"No silver," Soames was gurgling, clapping his hands together. "No silver, no silver, no silver..."

To Geller, it was as if he stood on the rim of the world. Not the bright rocky world of Luna, but the warm rich world of wealth. The little fork vibrating in his fist would decide whether he would go to that world, or be forever lost in the void of being nothing and nobody.

The vibrations were dying away. Geller began to pray, softly, fervently, the only way he knew.

"Goddam you, open up...open up...goddam you...open..."

And a counterweight creaked and a piece of rock moved.

Pile upon silver square pile it stood, delicately balanced, making a sheen that filled the hollow rock. Geller stepped back and laughed, loudly and happily, examining the beauty of it. The hoard...*Lachlin's silver!*

He seized Soames by the arm. "Start carrying those ingots to the ship." Everything had to be done quickly now, methodically.

SOAMES hefted several of the bars, nearly weightless in the reduced gravity. He started down the slope, stumbled once, got up, looked back at Geller, and vanished into the ship.

Geller felt coldness on his back. Those eyes no longer belonged to Soames. They belonged to something else...something that was driven into madness by the fear and the awful splendor of the rising mountains.

He drew his gun and waited. But Soames reappeared and labored up the hill. Together, then, they began to carry down more ingots.

Geller emerged from the rocket at the end of the third trip to see Soames standing rigidly at the top of the long slope.

"What's wrong?" Geller asked through the phone.

"Look there," Soames breathed. *"Look there!"*

Geller twisted. A rocket was rising from New Taos.

"They're after us," Soames was saying. "They're after us, Geller."

"That's the mail rocket! Probably sent out just now to bring help. They have no force in New Taos. They can't stop us."

He kept quiet. Soames was lifting one of the silver ingots high over his head. "They're coming for us," his voice creaked through the phone as if it sounded from some ancient grave. "I'm not going to help you any more..."

His arms came down and the ingot flashed free, spiraling toward Geller's head. Soames reached for another bar.

Throwing the silver away, thought Geller. *Throwing it away...*

He fired up the slope. Soames fell. He kept on firing. The bullets spanged into the stacked ingots. The precision balance of the silver was broken. They began to move. The piles buckled. Ingots mushroomed outward, past the body of Soames.

More and more of them tumbled from the crypt. They rolled down the hill in great silver waves.

Geller stood at the edge of the plateau, watching them, nearly hypnotized by the eye-shattering brilliance.

Suddenly, he screamed and turned and ran for the ship.

But the first of the ingots struck him and he staggered. The avalanche slammed against his body. He felt himself carried backward, flung out into space in the middle of turning metallic confusion.

He stopped screaming and watched the silver bars spin all around him. Their momentum carried him out and down, in a kind of unreal floating gravitational pull. The Burning Finger fell away in the sky.

He was still watching the Burning Finger when the fall ended. He felt a rock pressing into his back, bending it.

His back bent double...and his body broke apart.

The Control Police came out in a flier and gathered up all of Lachlin's twenty-eight year old hoard, from where it was strewn on the pumice plain. They took the body of Soames from the Burning Finger. One of them commented, as Earthmen always did when looking at the Leibnitz Mountains of the moon reaching into the night sky, that anyone would be a fool to try and conquer that awful majesty.

They had found all of the silver, and only a few scattered pieces of something once called Geller.

They climbed back into the flier. It rose in the bleak sky, a tiny spot against the mountains. The Burning Finger watched with eternal white strength.

THE END

To Remember Charlie By

By ROGER DEE

Just a one-eyed dog named Charlie and a crippled boy named Joey—but between them they changed the face of the universe...perhaps.

The history of this materialistic world is highlighted with strange events that scientists and historians, unable to explain logically, have dismissed with such labels as "supernatural," "miracle," etc. But there are those among us whose simple faith can—and often does—alter the scheme of the universe. Even a little child can do it...

I NEARLY STUMBLED over the kid in the dark before I saw him.

His wheelchair was parked as usual on the tired strip of carpet grass that separated his mother's trailer from the one Doc Shull and I lived in, but it wasn't exactly where I'd learned to expect it when I rolled in at night from the fishing boats. Usually it was nearer the west end of the strip where Joey could look across the crushed-shell square of the Twin Palms trailer court and the palmetto flats to the Tampa highway beyond. But this time it was pushed back into the shadows away from the court lights.

The boy wasn't watching the flats tonight, as he usually did. Instead he was lying back in his chair with his face turned to the sky, staring upward with such absorbed intensity that he didn't even know I was there until I spoke.

"Anything wrong, Joey?" I asked.

He said, "No, Roy," without taking his eyes off the sky.

For a minute I had the prickly feeling you get when you are watching a movie and find that you know just what is going to happen next. You're puzzled and a little spooked until you realize that the reason you can predict the action so exactly is because you've seen the same thing happen somewhere else a long time ago. I forgot the feeling when I remembered why the kid wasn't

46

watching the palmetto flats. But I couldn't help wondering why he'd turned to watching the sky instead.

"What're you looking for up there, Joey?" I asked.

He didn't move and from the tone of his voice I got the impression that he only half heard me.

"I'm moving some stars," he said softly.

I gave it up and went on to my own trailer without asking any more fool questions. How can you talk to a kid like that?

Doc Shull wasn't in, but for once I didn't worry about him. I was trying to remember just what it was about my stumbling over Joey's wheelchair that had given me that screwy double-exposure feeling of familiarity. I got a can of beer out of the ice-box because I think better with something cold in my hand, and by the time I had finished the beer I had my answer.

The business I'd gone through with Joey outside was familiar because it had happened before, about six weeks back when Doc and I first parked our trailer at the Twin Palms court. I'd nearly stumbled over Joey that time too, but he wasn't moving stars then. He was just staring ahead of him, waiting.

He'd been sitting in his wheelchair at the west end of the carpet-grass strip, staring out over the palmetto flats, toward the highway. He was practically holding his breath, as if he was waiting for somebody special to show up, so absorbed in his watching that he didn't know I was there until I spoke. He reminded me a little of a ventriloquist's dummy with his skinny, knob-kneed body, thin face and round, still eyes. Only there wasn't anything comical about him the way there is about a dummy. Maybe that's why I spoke, because he looked so deadly serious.

"Anything wrong, kid?" I asked.

He didn't jump or look up. His voice placed him as a cracker, either south Georgian or native Floridian.

"I'm waiting for Charlie to come home," he said, keeping his eyes on the highway.

Probably I'd have asked who Charlie was but just then the trailer door opened behind him and his mother took over.

I couldn't see her too well because the lights were off inside the trailer. But I could tell from the way she filled up the doorway that she was big. I could make out the white blur of a cigarette in her mouth, and when she struck a match to light it—on her thumbnail, like a man—I saw that she was fairly young and not bad-looking in a tough, sullen sort of way. The wind was blowing in my direction and it told me she'd had a drink recently, gin, by the smell of it.

"This is none of your business, mister," she said. Her voice was Southern like the boy's but with all the softness ground out of it from living on the Florida coast where you hear a hundred different accents everyday. "Let the boy alone."

She was right about it being none of my business. I went on into the trailer I shared with Doc Shull and left the two of them waiting for Charlie together.

Our trailer was dark inside, which meant first that Doc had probably gone out looking for a drink as soon as I left that morning to pick up a job, and second that he'd probably got too tight to find his way back. But I was wrong on at least one count, because when I switched on the light and dumped the packages I'd brought on the sink cabinet I saw Doc asleep in his bunk.

He'd had a drink, though. I could smell it on him when I shook him awake, and it smelled like gin.

Doc sat up and blinked against the light, a thin, elderly little man with bright blue eyes, a clipped brown mustache and scanty brown hair touseled and wild from sleep. He was stripped to his shorts against the heat, but at some time during the day he had bathed and shaved. He had even washed and ironed a shirt; it hung on a nail over his bunk with a crumpled pack of cigarettes in the pocket.

"Crawl out and cook supper, Rip," I said, holding him to his end of our working agreement. "I've made a day and I'm hungry."

Doc got up and stepped into his pants. He padded barefoot across the linoleum and poked at the packages on the sink cabinet.

"Snapper steak again," he complained. "Roy, I'm sick of fish!"

"You don't catch sirloins with a hand-line," I told him. And because I'd never been able to stay sore at him for long I added, "But we got beer. Where's the opener?"

"I'm sick of beer, too," Doc said. "I need a real drink."

I sniffed the air, making a business of it. "You've had one already. Where?"

He grinned at me then with the wise-to-himself-and-the-world grin that lit up his face like turning on a light inside and made him different from anybody else on earth.

"The largess of Providence," he said, "is bestowed impartially upon sot and Samaritan. I helped the little fellow next door to the bathroom this afternoon while his mother was away at work, and my selflessness had its just reward."

Sometimes it's hard to tell when Doc is kidding. He's an educated man—used to teach at some Northern college, he said once, and I never doubted it—and talks like one when he wants to. But Doc's no bum, though he's a semi-alcoholic and lets me support him like an invalid uncle, and he's keen enough to read my mind like a racing form.

"No, I didn't batter down the cupboard and help myself," he said. "The lady—her name is Mrs. Ethel Pond—gave me the drink. Why else do you suppose I'd launder a shirt?"

That was like Doc. He hadn't touched her bottle though his insides were probably snarled up like barbed wire for the want of it. He'd shaved and pressed a shirt instead so he'd look decent enough to rate a shot of gin she'd offer him as a reward. It wasn't such a doubtful gamble at that, because Doc has a way with him when he bothers to use it; maybe that's why he bums around with me after the commercial fishing and migratory crop work, because he's used that charm too often in the wrong places.

"Good enough," I said and punctured a can of beer apiece for us while Doc put the snapper steaks to cook.

He told me more about our neighbors while we killed the beer. The Ponds were permanent residents. The kid—his name was Joey and he was ten—was a polio case who hadn't walked for over a year, and his mother was a waitress at a roadside joint named the Sea Shell Diner. There wasn't any Mr. Pond. I guessed there never had been, which would explain why Ethel acted so tough and sullen.

We were halfway through supper when I remembered something the kid had said.

"Who's Charlie?" I asked.

Doc frowned at his plate. "The kid had a dog named Charlie, a big shaggy mutt with only one eye and no love for anybody but the boy. The dog isn't coming home. He was run down by a car on the highway while Joey was hospitalized with polio."

"Tough," I said, thinking of the kid sitting out there all day in his wheelchair, straining his eyes across the palmetto flats. "You mean he's been waiting a *year?*"

Doc nodded, seemed to lose interest in the Ponds, so I let the subject drop. We sat around after supper and polished off the rest of the beer. When we turned in around midnight I figured we wouldn't be staying long at the Twin Palms trailer court. It wasn't a very comfortable place.

I was wrong there. It wasn't comfortable, but we stayed.

I couldn't have said at first why we stuck, and if Doc could he didn't volunteer. Neither of us talked about it. We just went on living the way we were used to living, a few weeks here and a few there, all over the States.

We'd hit the Florida west coast too late for the citrus season, so I went in for the fishing instead. I worked the fishing boats all the way from Tampa down to Fort Myers, not signing on with any of the commercial companies because I like to move quick when I get restless. I picked the independent deep-water snapper runs mostly, because the percentage is good there if you've got a strong back and tough hands.

Snapper fishing isn't the sport it seems to the one-day tourists who flock along because the fee is cheap. You fish from a wide-beamed old scow, usually, with hand-lines instead of regular tackle, and you use multiple hooks that go down to the bottom where the big red ones are. There's no real thrill to it, as the one-day anglers find out quickly. A snapper puts up no more fight than a catfish and the biggest job is to haul out his dead weight once you've got him surfaced.

Usually a pro like me sells his catch to the boat's owner or to some clumsy sport who wants his picture shot with a big one, and there's nearly always a jackpot—from a pool made up at the beginning of every run—for the man landing the biggest fish of the day. There's a knack to hooking the big ones, and when the jackpots were running good I only worked a day or so a week and spent the rest of the time lying around the trailer playing cribbage and drinking beer with Doc Shull.

Usually it was the life of Riley, but somehow it wasn't enough in this place. We'd get about half-oiled and work up a promising argument about what was wrong with the world. Then, just when we'd got life looking its screwball funniest with our arguments one or the other of us would look out the window and see Joey Pond in his wheelchair, waiting for a one-eyed dog named Charlie to come trotting home across the palmetto flats. He was always there, day or night, until his mother came home from work and rolled him inside.

It wasn't right or natural for a kid to wait like that for anything and it worried me. I even offered once to buy the kid another mutt but Ethel Pond told me quick to mind my own business. Doc explained that the kid didn't want another mutt because he had what Doc called a psychological block.

"Charlie was more than just a dog to him," Doc said. "He was a sort of symbol because he offered the kid two things that no one else in the world could—security and independence. With Charlie keeping him company he felt secure, and he was independent of the kids who could run and play because he had Charlie to play with. If he took another dog now he'd be giving up more than Charlie. He'd be giving up everything that Charlie had meant to him, then there wouldn't be any point in living."

I could see it when Doc put it that way. The dog had spent more time with Joey than Ethel had, and the kid felt as safe with him as he'd have been with a platoon of Marines. And Charlie, being a one-man dog, had depended on Joey for the affection he wouldn't take from anybody else. The dog needed Joey and Joey needed him. Together, they'd been a natural.

At first I thought it was funny that Joey never complained or cried when Charlie didn't come home, but Doc explained that it was all a part of this psychological block business. If Joey cried he'd be admitting that Charlie was lost. So he waited and watched, secure in his belief that Charlie would return.

The Ponds got used to Doc and me being around, but they never got what you'd call intimate. Joey would laugh at some of the droll things Doc said, but his eyes always went back to the palmetto flats and the highway, looking for Charlie. And he never let anything interfere with his routine.

That routine started every morning when old man Cloehessey, the postman, pedaled his bicycle out from Twin Palms to leave a handful of mail for the trailer-court tenants. Cloehessey would always make it a point to ride back by way of the Pond trailer and Joey would stop him and ask if he's seen anything of a one-eyed dog on his route that day.

Old Cloehessey would lean on his bike and take off his sun helmet and mop his bald scalp, scowling while he pretended to think.

Then he'd say, "Not today, Joey," or, "Thought so yesterday, but this fellow had two eyes on him. 'Twasn't Charlie."

Then he'd pedal away, shaking his head. Later on the handyman would come around to swap sanitary tanks under the trailers and Joey would ask him the same question. Once a month the power company sent out a man to read the electric meters and he was part of Joey's routine too.

It was hard on Ethel. Sometimes the kid would dream at night that Charlie had come home and was scratching at the trailer ramp to be let in, and he'd wake Ethel and beg her to go out and see. When that happened Doc and I could hear Ethel talking to him, low and steady, until all hours of the morning, and when he finally went back to sleep we'd hear her open the cupboard and take out the gin bottle.

But there came a night that was more than Ethel could take, a night that changed Joey's routine and a lot more with it. It left a mark you've seen yourself—everybody has that's got eyes to see— though you never knew what made it. Nobody ever knew that but Joey and Ethel Pond and Doc and me.

Doc and I were turning in around midnight that night when the kid sang out next door. We heard Ethel get up and go to him, and we got up too and opened a beer because we knew neither of us would sleep any more till she got Joey quiet again. But this night was different. Ethel hadn't talked to the kid long when he yelled, "Charlie! *Charlie!*" and after that we heard both of them bawling.

A little later Ethel came out into the moonlight and shut the trailer door behind her. She looked rumpled and beaten, her hair straggling damply on her shoulders and her eyes puffed and red from crying. The gin she'd had hadn't helped any either.

She stood for a while without moving, then she looked up at the sky and said something I'm not likely to forget.

"Why couldn't You give the kid a break?" she said, not railing or anything but loud enough for us to hear. "You, up there— what's another lousy one-eyed mutt to You?"

Doc and I looked at each other in the half-dark of our own trailer. "She's done it, Roy," Doc said.

I knew what he meant and wished I didn't. Ethel had finally told the kid that Charlie wasn't coming back, not ever.

That's why I was worried about Joey when I came home the next evening and found him watching the sky instead of the palmetto flats. It meant he'd given up waiting for Charlie. And the quiet way the kid spoke of moving the stars around worried me more, because it sounded outright crazy.

Not that you could blame him for going off his head. It was tough enough to be pinned to a wheelchair without being able to wiggle so much as a toe. But to lose his dog in the bargain…

I was on my third beer when Doc Shull rolled in with a big package under his arm. Doc was stone sober, which surprised me, and he was hot and tired from a shopping trip to Tampa, which surprised me more. It was when he ripped the paper off his package, though, that I thought he'd lost his mind.

"Books for Joey," Doc said. "Ethel and I agreed this morning that the boy needs another interest to occupy his time now, and since he can't go to school I'm going to teach him here."

He went on to explain that Ethel hadn't had the heart the night before, desperate as she was, to tell the kid the whole truth. She'd told him instead, quoting an imaginary customer at the Sea Shell Diner, that a tourist car with Michigan license plates had picked Charlie up on the highway and taken him away. It was a good enough story. Joey still didn't know that Charlie was dead, but his waiting was over because no dog could be expected to find his way home from Michigan.

"We've got to give the boy another interest," Doc said, putting away the books and puncturing another beer can. "Joey has a remarkable talent for concentration—most handicapped children have—that could be the end of him if it isn't diverted into safe channels."

I thought the kid had cracked up already and said so.

"Moving stars?" Doc said when I told him. "Good Lord, Roy—"

Ethel Pond knocked just then, interrupting him. She came in and had a beer with us and talked to Doc about his plan for educating Joey at home. But she couldn't tell us anything more about the kid's new fixation than we already knew. When she asked him why he stared up at the sky like that he'd say only that he wants something to remember Charlie by.

It was about nine o'clock, when Ethel went home to cook supper. Doc and I knocked off our cribbage game and went outside with our folding chairs to get some air. It was then that the first star moved.

It moved all of a sudden, the way any shooting star does, and shot across the sky in a curving, blue-white streak of fire. I didn't pay much attention, but Doc nearly choked on his beer.

"Roy," he said, "that was Sirius! *It moved!*"

I didn't see anything serious about it and said so. You can see a dozen or so stars zip across the sky on any clear night if you're in the mood to look up.

"Not serious, you fool," Doc said. "The *star* Sirius—the Dog Star, it's called—it moved a good sixty degrees, *then stopped dead.*"

I sat up and took notice then, partly because the star really had stopped instead of burning out the way a falling star seems to do, partly because anything that excites Doc Shull that much is something to think about.

We watched the star like two cats at a mouse-hole, but it didn't move again. After a while a smaller one did, though, and later in the night a whole procession of them streaked across the sky and fell into place around the first one, forming a pattern that didn't make any sense to us. They stopped moving around midnight and we went to bed, but neither of us got to sleep right away.

"Maybe we ought to look for another interest in life ourselves instead of drumming up one for Joey," Doc said. He meant it as a joke but it had a shaky sound. "Something besides getting beered up every night, for instance."

"You think we've got the d.t.'s from drinking *beer?*" I asked.

Doc laughed at that, sounding more like his old self. "No, Roy. No two people ever had instantaneous and identical hallucinations."

"Look," I said, "I know this sounds crazy but maybe Joey—"

Doc wasn't amused any more. "Don't be a fool, Roy. If those stars really moved you can be sure of two things—Joey had nothing to do with it, and the papers will explain everything tomorrow."

He was wrong on one count at least.

The papers next day were packed with scareheads three inches high but none of them explained anything. The radio commentators quoted every authority they could reach, and astronomers were going crazy everywhere. It just couldn't happen, they said.

Doc and I went over the news column by column that night and I learned more about the stars than I'd learned in a lifetime. Doc, as I've said before, is an educated man, and what he couldn't recall offhand about astronomy the newspapers quoted by chapter and verse. They ran interviews with astronomers at Harvard Observatory and Mount Wilson and Lick and Flagstaff and God knows where else, but nobody could explain why all of those stars would change position then stop.

It set me back on my heels to learn that Sirius was twice as big as the Sun and more than twice as heavy, that it was three times as hot and had a little dark companion that was more solid than lead but didn't give off enough light to be seen with the naked eye. This little companion—astronomers called it the "Pup" because Sirius was the Dog Star—hadn't moved, which puzzled the astronomers no end. I suggested to Doc, only half joking, that maybe the Pup had stayed put because it wasn't bright enough to suit Joey's taste, but Doc called me down sharp.

"Don't joke about Joey," he said sternly. "Getting back to Sirius—it's so far away that its light needs eight and a half years to reach us. That means it started moving when Joey was only eighteen months old. The speed of light is a universal constant, Roy, and astronomers say it can't be changed."

"They said the stars couldn't be tossed around like pool balls, too," I pointed out. "I'm not saying that Joey really moved those damn stars, Doc, but if he did he could have moved the light along with them, couldn't he?"

But Doc wouldn't argue the point. "I'm going out for air," he said.

I trailed along, but we didn't get farther than Joey's wheelchair.

There he sat, tense and absorbed, staring up at the night sky. Doc and I followed his gaze, the way you do automatically when somebody on the street ahead of you cranes his neck at something. We looked up just in time to see the stars start moving again.

The first one to go was a big white one that slanted across the sky like a Roman candle fireball—*zip*, like that—and stopped dead beside the group that had collected around Sirius.

Doc said, "There went Altair," and his voice sounded like he had just run a mile.

That was only the beginning. During the next hour forty or fifty more stars flashed across the sky and joined the group that had moved the night before. The pattern they made still didn't look like anything in particular.

I left Doc shaking his head at the sky and went over to give Joey, who had called it a night and was hand-rolling his wheelchair toward the Pond trailer, a boost up the entrance ramp. I pushed him inside where Doc couldn't hear, then I asked him how things were going.

"Slow, Roy," he said. "I've got most a hundred to go, yet."

"Then you're really moving those stars up there?"

He looked surprised. "Sure, it's not so hard once you know how."

The odds were even that he was pulling my leg, but I went ahead anyway and asked another question.

"I can't make head or tail of it, Joey," I said. "What're you making up there?"

He gave me a very small smile. "You'll know when I'm through," he said.

I told Doc about that after we'd bunked in, but he said I should not encourage the kid in his crazy thinking. "Joey's heard everybody talking about those stars moving, the radio newscasters blared about it, so he's excited too. But he's got a lot more imagination than most people, because he's a cripple, and he could go off on a crazy tangent because he's upset about Charlie. The thing to do is give him a logical explanation instead of letting him think his fantasy is a fact."

Doc was taking all this so hard because it was upsetting things he'd taken for granted as being facts all his life, like those astronomers who were going nuts in droves all over the world. I didn't realize how upset Doc really was, though, till he woke me up at about 4:00 A.M.

"I can't sleep for thinking about those stars," he said, sitting on the edge of my bunk. "Roy, I'm *scared.*"

That from Doc was something I'd never expected to hear. It startled me wide enough awake to sit up in the dark and listen while he unloaded his worries.

"I'm afraid," Doc said, "because what is happening up there isn't right or natural. It just can't be, yet it is."

It was so quiet when he paused that I could hear the blood swishing in my ears. Finally Doc said, "Roy, the galaxy we live in is as delicately balanced as a fine watch. If that balance is upset too far our world will be affected drastically."

Ordinarily I wouldn't have argued with Doc on his own ground, but I could see he was painting a mental picture of the whole universe crashing together like a Fourth of July fireworks display and I was afraid to let him go on.

"The trouble with you educated people," I said, "is that you think your experts have got everything figured out, that there's nothing in the world their slide-rules can't pin down. Well, I'm an illiterate mugg, but I know that your astronomers can measure the stars till they're blue in the face and they'll never learn who *put* those stars there. So how do they know that whoever put them there won't move them again? I've always heard that if a man had faith enough he could move mountains. Well, if a man has the faith in himself that Joey's got maybe he could move stars, too."

Doc sat quiet for a minute.

"*There are more things, Horatio...*" he began, then laughed. "A line worn threadbare by three hundred years of repetition but as apt tonight as ever, Roy. Do you really believe Joey is moving those stars?"

"Why not?" I came back. "It's as good an answer as any the experts have come up with."

Doc got up and went back to his own bunk. "Maybe you're right. We'll find out tomorrow."

And we did. Doc did, rather, while I was hard at work hauling red snappers up from the bottom of the Gulf.

I got home a little earlier than usual that night, just before it got really dark. Joey was sitting as usual all alone in his wheelchair. In the gloom I could see a stack of books on the grass beside him, books Doc had given him to study. The thing that stopped me was that Joey was staring at his feet as if they were the first ones he'd ever seen, and he had the same look of intense concentration on his face that I'd seen when he was watching the stars.

I didn't know what to say to him, thinking maybe I'd better not mention the stars. But Joey spoke first.

"Roy," he said, without taking his eyes off his toes, "did you know that Doc is an awfully wise man?"

I said I'd always thought so, but why?

"Doc said this morning that I ought not to move any more stars," the kid said. "He says I ought to concentrate instead on learning how to walk again so I can go to Michigan and find Charlie."

For a minute I was mad enough to brain Doc Shull if he'd been handy. Anybody that would pull a gag like that on a crippled, helpless kid...

"Doc says that if I can do what I've been doing to the stars then it ought to be easy to move my own feet," Joey said. "And he's right, Roy. So I'm not going to move any more stars. I'm going to move my feet."

He looked up at me with his small, solemn smile. "It took me a whole day to learn how to move that first star, Roy, but I could do this after only a couple of hours. Look..."

And he wiggled the toes on both feet.

It's a pity things don't happen in life like they do in books, because a first-class story could be made out of Joey Pond's knack for moving things by looking at them. In a book Joey might have saved the world or destroyed it, depending on which line would interest the most readers and bring the writer the fattest check, but of course it didn't really turn out either way. It ended in what Doc Shull called an anticlimax, leaving everybody happy enough except a few astronomers who like mysteries anyway or they wouldn't be astronomers in the first place.

The stars that had been moved stayed where they were, but the pattern they had started was never finished. That unfinished pattern won't ever go away, in case you've wondered about it—it's up there in the sky where you can see it any clear night—but it will never be finished because Joey Pond lost interest in it when he learned to walk again.

Walking was a slow business with Joey at first because his legs had got thin and weak—partially atrophied muscles, Doc said and it took time to make them round and strong again. But in a couple of weeks he was stumping around on crutches and after that he never went near his wheelchair again.

Ethel sent him to school at Sarasota by bus and before summer vacation time came around he was playing softball and fishing in the Gulf with a gang of other kids on Sundays.

School opened up a whole new world to Joey and he fitted himself into the routine as neat as if he'd been doing it all his life. He learned a lot there and he forgot a lot that he'd learned for himself by being alone. Before we realized what was happening he was just like any other ten-year old, full of curiosity and the devil, with no more power to move things by staring at them than anybody else had.

I think he actually forgot about those stars along with other things that had meant so much to him when he was tied to his wheelchair and couldn't do anything but wait and think.

For instance, a scrubby little terrier followed him home from Twin Palms one day and Ethel let him keep it. He fed the pup and washed it and named it Dugan, and after that he never said anything more about going to Michigan to find Charlie. It was only natural, of course, because kids—normal kids—forget their pain quickly. It's a sort of defense mechanism, Doc says, against the disappointments of this life.

When school opened again in the fall Ethel sold her trailer and got a job in Tampa where Joey could walk to school instead of going by bus. When they were gone the Twin Palms trailer court was so lonesome and dead that Doc and I pulled out and went down to the Lake Okeechobee country for the sugar cane season. We never heard from Ethel and Joey again.

We've moved several times since; we're out in the San Joaquin Valley just now, with the celery croppers. But everywhere we go we're reminded of them. Every time we look up at a clear night sky we see what Doc calls the Joey Pond Stellar Monument, which is nothing but a funny sort of pattern roughed in with a hundred or so stars of all sizes and colors.

The body of it is so sketchy that you'd never make out what it's supposed to be unless you knew already what you were looking for. To us the head of a dog is fairly plain. If you know enough to fill in the gaps you can see it was meant to be a big shaggy dog with only one eye.

Doc says that footloose migratories like him and me forget old associations as quick as kids do—and for the same good reason— so I'm not especially interested now in where Ethel and Joey Pond are or how they're doing. But there's one thing I'll always wonder about, now that there's no way of ever knowing for sure.

I wish I'd asked Joey or Ethel, before they moved away, how Charlie lost that other eye.

THE END

All Jackson's Children

By DANIEL F. GALOUYE

Their chances hung literally on a prayer...which they had to answer all by themselves!

ANGUS McINTOSH vigorously scuffed the tarnished nameplate on the wrecked cargo carrier. Then he stepped back and squinted under shaggy gray eyebrows.

Letter by letter, number by number, he coaxed out the designation on the crumpled bow of the spacer in the vine-matted gorge: "RT...3070...VG-II."

His lean frame tensed with concern as he turned to stare soberly at the other. "A Vegan robot trader!"

Bruce Drummond grinned. "Are we lucky? Clunkers are worth money—in any condition."

Angus snorted impatiently. "Let's get out of here, quick."

"Get out?" the stocky Drummond repeated incredulously as he ran thickset fingers over the black stubble on his cheek. "Ain't we going to salvage the clunkers? The book says they're ours after fifty years."

"The hold's empty. There's no cargo."

"There was when it landed. Look at the angle of incidence on those fins."

"Exactly." Frowning, Angus shifted his holster around on his hip and strode back toward the plain. "Ever hear of a frustrated compulsion?"

DRUMMOND, following hesitantly, shook his head.

"Those clunkers have to satisfy a basic behavior circuit," McIntosh explained as he hastened his step. "We don't know what the compulsion of this bunch is. Suppose—well, suppose they have a chiropractic function. How'd you like to be the first person to show up after they've been frustrated for a hundred years?"

"Oh," Drummond said comprehendingly, stumbling to keep pace.

Angus McIntosh brushed a mass of tendrils aside and stepped out on the plain. "We'll report it and let them send in a deactivation crew. That way, at least, we'll get fifty percent of salvage and no danger."

"Even that ain't bad—just for following an SOS a hundred light-years. Taking an uncharted route and picking up that signal sure paid off like—"

Drummond gagged on his words as he gripped Angus's arm and pointed.

Their ship was a shining oval, bobbing and weaving on a sea of silver that surged across the plain toward a cliff on the left.

"Clunkers," Drummond gasped. "Hundreds of 'em—making off with our boat!"

He unholstered his weapon and fired.

Angus struck his wrist sharply. "Why don't you just run out waving your arms? We don't have enough firepower to get more than eight or ten of them."

But the warning was too late. Already the tide had washed away from the ship and was surging toward the gorge.

There was a noise behind them and Angus spun around. Ten feet away stood a robot with the designation RA-204 on his breastplate.

"Welcome, O Jackson," the clunker said reverently.

Then he hinged forward on his hip joints until his head almost touched the ground. The gesture was a clockwork salaam.

McINTOSH'S thin legs dangled in front of 204's breastplate and his ankles were secure in the grip of metal fingers as he rode the robot's shoulders.

RA-76 strode alongside, carrying a squirming and swearing Drummond. Around them, the shining horde marched along noisily.

"He has come!" cried one.

"Jackson has come!" chanted the others of the shining horde.

"He will show us the way!" shouted RA-204.

Drummond kicked, but 76 only held his legs more firmly. Furious, Drummond reached for his gun.

"That's using your head," Angus said sarcastically. "Agitate them. Then we'll never get out of here."

Drummond let the weapon slip back into its holster. "What did we get into—a nest of fanatics? Who's Jackson?"

Angus helplessly shrugged his bony shoulders.

The procession filtered through a narrow woods and broke out on another plain, headed for the nearby cliff.

Angus leaned forward. "Put me down, 204."

"Thou art Jackson," said the robot solemnly. "And Thou art testing me to see whether I would so easily abandon my Supervisor."

"Not testing," Angus said. "Just asking. Come on, how about it?"

"Praise Jackson!" 204 cried.

"Jackson! Jackson!" intoned the throng.

Drummond leaned an elbow on 76's skull plate and disgustedly cupped his chin in his hand. "What if they are chiropractor robots?"

"We'll probably need one after this ride," Angus said uncomfortably.

"Not like we'll need a way to get back to the ship and cut off those converters before they overcharge."

"Slow charge?" Angus asked between grunts timed with 204's stride.

"Hell, no. I didn't think we'd be here more than a couple of hours. By tomorrow at this time, there'll be a crater out there big enough to bury the Capellan fleet."

"Great," said Angus. "That gives us another thing to worry about."

The robots fell into two groups as they neared a cave in the cliff.

"Jackson is my Supervisor!" chanted the ones on the right.

"I shall not rust!" answered those on the left.

"He maketh me to adjust my joint tension!" cried the first group.

"Oh, brother," said Drummond.

"Sounds like a psalm," suggested Angus.

"You ought to know. You always got your nose in that Bible."

"Notice anything peculiar about them?"

"Very funny," sneered Drummond at the question.

"No, I'm serious."

"They bounce the daylights out of you when they walk," Drummond grumbled.

"No. Their finish. It's shiny—like they were fresh out of the factory—not like they've been marooned here for a hundred years."

DRUMMOND scratched his chin. "Maybe their compulsion is metal polishing."

"Not with the kind of fingers they have."

Angus indicated the hand that held his ankle. Three digits were wrenches of various sizes. The index finger was a screwdriver. The thumb was a Stillson wrench. The thumb on the other hand was a disc-like appendage.

Drummond hunched over. "76, what's your function?"

The robot looked up. "To serve Jackson."

"You're a big help," said Drummond.

"Why dost thou tempt us, O Jackson?" asked RA-204. "Wouldst Thou test our beliefs?"

"We're no gods," Angus declared as the robot drew up before the cave.

"Thou art Jackson!" insisted 204.

Drummond and McIntosh were hoisted to a ledge beside the mouth of the cave. The robots backed off, forming a half circle, and bowed in obeisance.

Angus ran a hand helplessly through his sparse gray hair. "Would you say there are four hundred of them?"

"At least." Drummond surveyed the expanse of metal bodies. "You know, maybe they don't have a function."

"Impossible. Hasn't been a clunker in five hundred years without a primary compulsion."

"Think they forgot theirs?"

"Can't. They may forget how to put it in words, but the compulsion is good for as long as their primary banks are intact. That's not what's worrying me, though."

"No?"

"*Religious* robots... There can't be any such brand. Yet here they are."

Drummond studied them silently.

"Before there can be theological beliefs," McIntosh went on, "there has to be some sort of foundation—the mystery of origin, the fear of death, the concept of the hereafter. Clunkers *know* they come from a factory. They *know* that when they're finally disassembled, they'll be lifeless scrap metal."

Drummond spat disdainfully. "One thing's for sure—this pack thinks we're God Almighty."

"Jackson Almighty," Angus corrected somberly.

"Well, God or Jackson, we'd better get back to the ship or this is going to be a long visitation."

Drummond faced the almost prostrate robots and made a megaphone of his hands. "All right, you guys! How's about knocking it off?"

Slowly, the robots reared erect, waiting.

"Take us back to our ship."

RA-204 stepped forward. "Again Thou art testing us, O Jackson."

ANGUS spread his arms imploringly. "Look, fellows. We're men. We're—"

"Thou art our Supervisor!" the throng roared.

"One of you is Jackson," explained 204. "The other is a Divine Test. We must learn which is the True Supervisor."

"You're *not* being tested," McIntosh insisted.

"Our beliefs are firm, O Jackson!" cried a hundred metallic voices.

"Thou are the Supervisor!" declared 204 resolutely.

"For God's sake," urged Drummond, "tell 'em you're their Jackson and then lay down the law."

"No. Can't do it that way."

"Why not? Unfair advantage, I suppose?" There was a cutting edge on the younger man's words.

Angus stared thoughtfully at the robots. "If we only knew how they forgot their origin, how they got religion, we might find a way to get through to them."

Drummond laughed contemptuously. *"You* figure it out. *I'm* going to play Jackson and get back to the ship." He turned toward the robots.

But McIntosh caught his arm. ' "Let me try something else first." He faced the horde below. "Who made you?"

"Thou hast, O Supervisor!" the robots chanted like a gleeful Sunday school class.

"And Thou hast put us on this world and robot begot robot until we were as we are today," added 204 solemnly.

Drummond slapped the heel of his hand against his forehead. "Now they think they've got a sex function!"

Angus's shoulders fell dismally. "Maybe if we try to figure out their designation. They're all Ras—whatever the A stands for."

There was a hollow rumbling in the cave that grew in volume until the cliff shook. Then a second group of robots emerged and fanned out to encircle the ledge.

"Hell," said Drummond in consternation. "There's twice as many as we figured."

"Thought there'd be more," Angus admitted. "That ship was big enough to hold a thousand clunkers. And they didn't waste space in those days."

The newcomers fell prostrate alongside the others.

THE planet's single satellite hung like a lost gem over the low mountains east of the plain. It washed the cliff with a cloak of effulgence and bathed the forbidden ship in an aura of gleaming silver.

Below the ledge, the reverent robots wavered occasionally and highlights of coruscation played capriciously across their plates. Their whispered invocations were a steady drone, like the soft touch of the wind.

"Quit it!" Drummond yelled angrily. "Break it up! Go home!"

Angus sat with his head against the cliff, face tilted up. "That didn't help any."

"When are they going to give up?"

McIntosh glanced abstractedly at the horde. "How long would we keep it up if *our* God appeared among us?"

Drummond swore. "Damned if you haven't been reading the print off that Bible…"

"What do you suppose happened," Angus went on heedlessly, "to make them more than clunkers—to make them grope for the basic truths?"

Drummond spat disgustedly in answer.

"Civilization goes on for a hundred years," Angus said as he leaned back and closed his eyes, "spreading across a hunk of the Galaxy, carrying along its knowledge and religious convictions. And all the while, there's this little lost island of mimic beliefs— so much like our own creed, except that their god is called Jackson."

Drummond rose and paced. "Well, you'll have plenty of time to set them straight, if we're still sitting on this shelf eleven hours from now."

"Maybe that's what it'll take—bringing them step by step through theology."

"Overnight?"

No, not overnight, Angus realized. It would take months to pound in new convictions.

Drummond slipped down from the ledge. "Here goes nothing."

Interestedly, Angus folded his arms and watched the other square his shoulders and march off confidently through the ranks of robots toward the ship in the distance.

For a moment, it seemed he would succeed. But two of the RAs suddenly reared erect and seized him by the arms. They bore him on their shoulders and deposited him back on the ridge beside McIntosh.

"Warm tonight," Drummond observed bitterly, glancing up at the sky.

"Sure is," Angus agreed, his voice calm. "Wouldn't be surprised if we got some rain tomorrow."

DRUMMOND flipped another pebble and it pinged down on a metal back. "Seven out of thirteen."

"Getting good."

"Look, let's tell 'em we're their Supervisor and end this marathon worship."

"Which one of us is going to play the divine role?"

"What difference does it make?"

Angus shrugged and his tired eyes stared off into the darkness. "One of us is—Jackson. The other is an impostor, brought here to test their faith. When they find out which is which, what are they going to do to the impostor?"

Drummond looked startled. "I see what you mean."

The miniature moon had wheeled its way to the zenith and now the first gray tinge of dawn silhouetted the peaks of the mountain range.

Angus rose and stretched. "We've got to find out what their function is."

"Why?"

"It looks like religion is their only interest. But maybe that's because they're completely frustrated in their basic compulsion. If we could discover their function, maybe we could focus their attention back on it."

"RA," Drummond mumbled puzzledly. "Robot agriculturist?"

ANGUS shook his head. "They wouldn't be frustrated—not with a whole planet to farm. Besides, they'd be equipped with agricultural implements instead of wrenches."

Drummond got up suddenly. "You figure it out. I have something else to try."

Angus followed him along the ledge until they reached the mouth of the cave.

"What are you going to do?"

Drummond hitched his trousers. "The way we're ringed in here, it's a cinch we won't get past 'em in the six hours we have left."

"So you're going to make off through the cave?"

The younger man nodded. "They might take off after me. That'll give you a chance to get to the ship and cut off those converters before they make like a nova."

Angus chuckled. "Suppose half of them decide to stay here with me?"

Drummond swore impatiently at his skepticism. "At any rate, one of us might get back to the converters."

"And leave the other here?"

"He can say he's Jackson and order an attack in force on the ship."

"I don't follow you."

"Skidding the ship in a circle with the exhaust blowers on," Drummond explained patiently, "will take care of *ten thousand* clunkers."

He dropped from the ledge and raced into the cave. None of the robots stirred. Either they hadn't noticed Drummond's departure, Angus reasoned, or they weren't concerned because they knew the cave led nowhere.

THE sun came up, daubing the cliff with splotches of orange and purple and striking up scintillations in the beads of dew on the robots' backs.

And still the tiresomely shouted veneration continued.

Angus paced the ledge, stopping occasionally to stare into the impenetrable shadows of the cave. He checked his watch. Five hours to go—five hours, and then time would be meaningless for the rest of his life with the ship destroyed.

It was unlikely that rescue would come. The wrecked spacer's automatic distress signals had gone out in an ever-expanding sphere for a hundred years, and he and Drummond had been the only humans to hear them.

Trade routes were pretty stable in this section of the Galaxy now. And it was hardly possible that, within the next ten or twenty years, one would be opened up that would intercept the SOS that had lured them here.

He stood up and surveyed the robots. "RA-204."

204 reared erect. "Yes, Jackson?"

"One of us is gone."

"We know, O Supervisor."

"Why did you let him get away?"

"If he is not the True Jackson, it doesn't matter that he fled. If he is the Supervisor, he will return. Otherwise, why did he come here to us in the first place?"

Another robot straightened. "We are ashamed, O Jackson, that we have failed the Divine Test and have not recognized our True Supervisor."

Angus held up his arms for silence. "Once there was a cargo of robots. That was a hundred years ago. The ship was from Vega II. It developed trouble and crashed when it tried to land on this planet. There was—"

"What's a year, O Supervisor?" asked 204.

"A Vega-two, Jackson?" said 76 bewilderedly.

"What's a planet?" another wanted to know.

McIntosh leaned back hopelessly against the cliff. All of their memories and a good deal of their vocabularies had been lost. He could determine how much only through days of conversation. It would take weeks to learn their function, to rekindle a sense of duty sufficiently strong to draw their interest away from religion. Unless—

He drew resolutely erect. "Strip the converters! Pull the aft tube lining!"

The robots looked uncomprehendingly at him. It was obvious they weren't trained for spacecraft maintenance.

But it had to have something to do with mechanics. "A battle fleet is orbiting at one diameter! Arm all warheads on the double!"

They stared helplessly at one another, then back at Angus. Not ordnance-men.

"Pedestrian Strip Number Two is jammed! Crane crew, muster on the right!"

The robots shifted uncertainly. Apparently they weren't civic maintenance-men, either.

Defeated, Angus scanned their blank faceplates. For a moment, it was almost as though he could discern expressions of confusion. Then he laughed at the thought that metal could accommodate a frown.

Suddenly the robots shifted their gaze to the cave. Drummond, shoulders sagging dismally, walked out and squinted against the glare. Several of the robots started toward him.

"Okay, okay!" he growled, heading back for the ledge before they could reach him.

"NO LUCK?" Angus asked. Disgusted, Drummond clambered up beside him. "The cave's just a nice-sized room."

"Took you two hours to find that out?"

The younger man shook his head. "I was hiding by the entrance, waiting for the clunkers to break it up and give me a chance to run for the ship... How many robots did we decide there were?"

"About eight hundred."

"Wrong. You can add another four hundred or so."

"In the cave?"

Drummond nodded. "With their parts spread all the way from here to hell and back."

"Dismantled?"

"Down to the last nut and bolt. They've even got their secondary memory banks stripped."

Angus was thoughtfully silent a long while. "RA..." he said finally. "Robot Assembler!"

"That's what I figured." Drummond turned back toward the robots and funneled his voice through his hands.

"Okay, you clunkers! I want all odd-numbered RAs stripped down for reconditioning!" He glanced at Angus. "When they get through, I'll have half of what's left strip the other half, and so forth."

McIntosh grinned caustically. "Brilliant! The whole operation shouldn't take more than two or three days." Then his face took on a grim cast. "Drummond, we've only got four hours left to get to those converters."

"But you don't understand. Once they get started, they'll be so busy, we'll probably be able to walk away."

Angus smiled indulgently. "Once they get started."

He nodded toward the robots.

They had all returned to their attitude of veneration.

"It won't work," McIntosh explained. "Their obsession with religion is stronger than their primary compulsion. That's probably because they've been satisfying their compulsion all along." He jerked a thumb in the direction of the cave.

Drummond swore venomously.

Angus dropped down on the ledge and folded his knees in his arms. He felt his age bearing down on him for the first time.

"Twelve hundred robots," he said meditatively. "Twelve hundred *RA* robots. Out of touch with civilization for a century. Satisfying their primary function by disassembling and assembling one another. Going at it in shifts. Splitting themselves into three groups."

"That device on their left thumb," Drummond interrupted. "It's a burnisher. That's why they're so shiny."

Angus nodded. "Three groups. Group A spends so many months stripping and reassembling Group B. Meanwhile, Group C, which has just been put together again, has no memory because their secondary banks have been wiped clean. So, like children, they learn from the working Group A."

DRUMMOND'S mouth hung open in shocked understanding. "And by the time A finishes the job, C's education is complete…and it's A's turn to be stripped."

"By then," Angus went on, "Group C is not only ready to start stripping Group A, but has also become intellectually mature enough to begin the education of the reassembled Group B."

They sat still for a while, thinking it over.

"The compulsion to do their jobs," McIntosh continued, "is unchanged because the primary function banks are sealed circuits and can't be tampered with. But in each generation, they have their secondary memory circuits wiped clean and have to start all over, getting whatever general knowledge they can from the last generation."

Drummond snapped his fingers excitedly. "That's why they don't know what we are. Their idea of Man had to be passed down by word of mouth. And it got all distorted in the process."

Angus's stare, more solicitous now, swept slowly over the prostrate robots. "More important, that's why they developed a religion. What's the main difference between human and robotic intelligence? It's that our span of life is limited on one end by birth, the other by death—mysteries of origin and destiny that can't be explained. You see, the ordinary clunker understands where he came from and where he's going. But

73

here are robots who have to struggle with those mysteries—birth and death of the conscious intellect, which they themselves once knew, and forgot, and now have turned into myths."

"So they start thinking in terms of religion," Drummond said. "Well, that clears up the whole thing, doesn't it?"

"Not quite. It doesn't explain why the religion they've invented parallels ours so closely. And it doesn't tell us who Jackson is."

Drummond ran thick fingernails against the stubble on his cheeks. "Jackson is my Supervisor, I shall not rust. He maketh me to adjust my joint tension—" He stopped and frowned. "I've heard that before somewhere, only it sounded different."

Angus gave him a wry, tired smile. "Sure. It's practically the Psalm of David. Now you see why the resemblance is driving me batty."

THE robots stirred. Several of them stood up and plodded into the cave. The others continued repeating their endless praise and devotion—prayers in every sense of the word except common sense.

Angus leaned back against the cliff and let the sun's heat warm him.

"Somehow it doesn't seem fair," he commented unhappily.

"What doesn't?" Drummond asked.

"They're so close to the Truth. Yet, after we file a report, a deactivation crew will come along and erase their beliefs. They'll have their memory banks swept clean and once more they'll be nothing but clunkers with a factory-specification job of routine work to do."

"Ain't that what they're supposed to be?"

"But these are different. They've found something no clunker's ever had before—hope, faith, aspiration beyond death." He shook his head ruefully.

There was movement at the mouth of the cave and the smaller group of robots emerged from the shadows, two of them bearing a stone slab. Their steps were ceremoniously slow as they approached the ledge. Bowing, they placed the tablet at Angus's feet and backed away.

"These are the articles of our faith, O Jackson," one announced. "We have preserved them for Thy coming."

McIntosh stared down at the charred remains of a book. Its metal-fiber binding was shredded and fused and encrusted with the dust of ages.

Drummond knelt beside it and, with stiff fingers, brushed away the film of grime, uncovering part of the title:

OLY
BIB E

Eagerly, Angus eased the cover back. Of the hundreds of pages it had originally contained, only flaked parts of two or three remained. The printing was scarcely legible on the moldy paper.

He read aloud those words he could discern:

"…to lie down in green pastures; He leadeth me beside cool waters; He…"

Drummond jabbed Angus with a triumphant forefinger. "They didn't invent any religion, after all!"

"It isn't important how they got it. The fact that they accepted it—that's what's important." McIntosh glanced up at Drummond. "They probably found this in the wreck of the ship they'd been in. It's easy to see they haven't used it in hundreds of generations. Instead, the gist of what's in it was passed down orally. And their basic concepts of Man and supervisor were distorted all along the way—confused with the idea of God."

GENTLY, he let the cover fall. And a shining square of duraloid fell out.

"It's somebody's picture," Drummond exclaimed.

"An ID card," Angus said, holding it so the light wouldn't reflect off its transparent protective cover.

It was a picture of a nondescript man—not as stout as Drummond, nor as lean as McIntosh—with hair neither all black, like the younger man's, nor nearly all white, like Angus's.

The print below the picture was indiscernible, except for the subject's last name…

"Jackson," Drummond whispered.

Angus slowly replaced the card. "A hundred years of false devotion," he said pensively. "Just think—"

"This is no time for that kind of gas." Drummond glanced at his watch. "We got just two hours to cut off those converters." Desperately, he faced the robots. "Hey, you clunkers! You're robot assemblers. You got four hundred clunkers in that cave, all in pieces. Get in there and put 'em together!"

Angus shook his head disapprovingly. Somehow it didn't seem right, calling them clunkers.

"Jackson is my Supervisor," intoned RA-204.

"Jackson is my Supervisor,' echoed the mass.

Drummond glanced frantically at his watch, then looked helplessly at Angus. Angus shrugged.

The younger man's face suddenly tensed with resolution. "So they've got to have a Jackson? All right, I'll *give* 'em one."

He waved his fist at the horde. I'm your Supervisor! I'm your Jackson! Now clear out of the way and—"

RA-76's hand darted out and seized Drummond's ankle, tugged him off the ledge. As he fell to the ground, a score of robots closed in over him, metal arms flailing down methodically. Angus yelled at them to stop, saw he was too late and sank down, turning away sickly.

Finally, after a long while, they backed off and faced Angus.

"We have passed the Divine test, O Jackson!" 204 shouted up jubilantly.

"We have redeemed ourselves before our Supervisor!" exclaimed 76.

It took a long, horror-filled moment before Angus could speak.

"How do you know?" he managed to ask at last.

"If he had been Jackson," exclaimed 204, "we could not have destroyed him."

THE robots fell prostrate again and returned to their devotional. But now the phrases were triumphant, where before they had been servile and uncertain.

Angus stared numbly down at Drummond, then backed against the cliff. The litany below exuberant now, grew mightily in volume, booming vibrantly against distant hills.

"There is but one Supervisor!" intoned 204.

"But one Jackson!" answered the assembly.

"And now He dwelleth among His children!" 76 chanted.

"In their midst!" boomed the hundreds.

Suddenly it all seemed horribly ludicrous and Angus laughed. The litany stopped and his laughter grew shriller, louder, edged with hysteria.

The shimmering sea of metal, confounded, stared at him and it was as though he could see fleshy furrows of confusion on the featureless faces... But how could a clunker show emotion?

His laughter slowed and died, like the passing of a violent storm. And he felt weakened with a sickening sense of compassion. Robots—*human* robots—standing awed before unknown concepts while they groped for Truth. Clunkers with a sense of right and wrong and with an overwhelming love. It was absurd that he had been elected father of twelve hundred children—whether flesh or metal—but it didn't *feel* at all absurd.

"Dost Thou despair of us, O Jackson?" asked 76 hesitantly, staring up at him.

204 motioned toward the ship, the top of its hull shining beyond the nearby woods. "Wouldst Thou *still* return to Thy vessel, Supervisor?"

Incredulous, Angus tensed. "You mean I can go?"

"If that is Thy wish, True Jackson, you may go," said 76 submissively.

As he watched unbelievingly, a corridor opened in their ranks, extending toward the woods and the ship beyond. He glanced anxiously at his watch. There was still more than an hour left.

Wearily, he dropped from the ledge and trudged toward freedom, trying to look straight ahead. His eyes, nevertheless, wandered to the dejected figures who faced him with their heads bowed.

Then he laughed again, realizing the illogical nature of his solicitous thoughts. Imagine—*dejected* clunkers! Still, the metal faces seemed somehow different. Where, a moment earlier, he had fancied expressions of jubilation, now there was the sense of hopelessness on the steel plates.

SHRUGGING off his uncertainty, he walked faster. After all, was it *his* fault they'd stumbled upon a substitute for birth and death and had become something more than clunkers? What was he supposed to do—stay and play missionary, bring them the Truth so that when a deactivation crew came along, they would be so advanced morally that no one would suggest their destruction?

He stopped and scanned the ranks on either side. He'd do one thing for them, at least—he wouldn't report the wreck. Then it would be centuries, probably, before another ship wandered far enough away from the trade routes to intercept the distress signals.

Relieved by his decision, he went ahead more at ease.

And the litany started again—softly, appealing:

"Jackson is my Supervisor."

"I shall not rust…"

Angus stiffened abruptly and stared at his watch, realizing belatedly that it had stopped. But how long ago? How much time did he have left? Should he take the chance and make a dash for the converters?

He reached the end of the robot corridor and started to spring for the ship.

But he halted and turned to glance back at the humble, patient horde . They were expectantly silent now…as though they could sense his indecision. He backed away from them.

Then the light of a hundred Arcturan days flared briefly and a mighty mountain of sound and concussion collapsed on him. The trees buckled and branches were hurled out against the cliff. It rained leaves and pieces of metal from the hull for a long while as Angus hugged the ground.

When he finally looked up, familier bits of the ship were strewn around him—a spacesuit helmet here, a control dial there, a transmitter tube up ahead.

He rose shakily, staring at a black book that lay near the helmet with its pages ruffled. He picked it up and straightened out the leaves. Then he motioned to the robots and they clustered around him.

He would have to start from the beginning.

He wet his lips.

"In the beginning," Angus read in a loud, convincing voice, **"God** created heaven and earth and the earth was void and empty and darkness was upon the face of the deep. And **God** said, 'Let there be light…'"

THE END

He Knew All the Answers

By DALLAS ROSS

What really happens when the lights go out? Does the sun remain when you close your eyes? In case of doubt, ask Jeremiah. He knows...

SUCH WAS Jeremiah Perkins' appearance and manner that nobody ever called him Jerry; not even his dear wife, Martha.

It occurred to him, one morning at breakfast that he had no reason to believe that the light stayed on when he closed his eyes and he expressed that opinion to Martha while between the editorial page and the financial section.

"What was that, dear?" she asked blearily. Martha was invariably bleary in the mornings, which was one of the factors contributing to Perkins' critical opinion of the connubial tie; another was that he had an antipathy for *large* women and Martha was rather more than twice his size, going pound for pound, of course, rather than by inches.

He enunciated clearly—and made it a point to *show* he was enunciating clearly—"I said that I have no reason to believe that the light stays on when I close my eyes."

"Oh." Martha went back to spreading a revoltingly thick layer of honey on her toast and Jeremiah Perkins returned to contemplation of the financial section.

"But, Jeremiah," his wife said finally. "Of course the light stays on when you close your eyes."

He lifted the eyes in question to hers and explained patiently, "I didn't say that it didn't, I merely stated that I have no reason to believe it does." His eyes went back to the stock market reports. "Which is an entirely different matter," he added.

Martha said weakly, "I don't believe I know *quite* what you mean, Jeremiah."

With an air of considerable patience, he put down the paper and stared at her through his heavy lensed pince-nez glasses. "Then I shall explain it very simply," he told her.

"You have possibly heard of persons who wondered whether or not the little light in the refrigerator remains on when the door of the refrigerator is closed."

"Oh, yes," Martha said with enthusiasm and, nodded her head until her chins wobbled disgustingly. "Mrs. Klatz was telling us a joke at the bridge club only last week about—"

He stared at her coldly and she stopped telling him about Mrs. Klatz and said, "Yes, dear."

He went on, "Now there are various ways in which it can be demonstrated to an even moderately lucid person that the light does indeed go out when the refrigerator door is shut. One recommended method is to put a small child into the refrigerator and close the door. However, this system depends upon the veracity of the child and I personally am not inclined to gullibility. Much better is to cut a small window in the door of the re-frigerator; then the person in doubt can himself observe what develops when the door of the refrigerator is closed. Do you understand thus far?"

She swallowed her current mouthful of honeyed bread hurriedly and said, "Yes, dear."

"Very well. Now my point was that while it can be proven satisfactorily that the light in the refrigerator does go off when the door is closed, I have no provable evidence that the light remains on when my eyes are closed."

She blinked at him, nearly spilling the cup of coffee she held in her plump right hand. He noted that, as usual, she'd filled her cup with quite as much heavy cream as with coffee.

He went on to elucidate further. "Suppose I enter a theatre during the day. What reason have I to believe that the sun remains on while I am inside?"

She offered hesitantly, "You could get up in the middle of the show and go and see."

Perkins snorted indignantly. "Don't you understand? If I did, by that time *they* would have turned it back on again."

He returned to his newspaper, closing the subject.

POSSIBLY the matter would have remained closed indefinitely had it not been for the fact that Mrs. Jeremiah Perkins noticed that her husband was evidently doing what he could in the way of checking upon his suspicions. For instance, that Sunday, while he was working down in the basement on his mushroom and toadstool collection, she noted that from time to time he would dash hurriedly up the stairs to peer disgustedly out the kitchen window.

At lunch he muttered, to no one in particular, "I nearly caught it yesterday when I got off the subway two stations before my stop and went up to the street."

Even then, Martha, who was a more than usually cautious wife when it came to these things—and don't think such matters hadn't come up before—would have done nothing if he'd just gone on for a time and then forgotten about it. The trouble was, he didn't forget; in fact, he got worse. He was continually devising situations in which he would be out of sight of the sun; in a theatre, in a subway, in the basement, in some room without a window, in the attic; then, abruptly, he'd make a sudden dash to check on whether or not the sun remained on while he was out of range of its beams.

He seemed disappointed when it invariably did.

One night when they were seated in the living room after dinner, she offered quietly, "Why would *they* want to turn the light out when your eyes are closed or when you're in the cellar or the attic?"

He had been rereading the Kinsey report but he looked up impatiently to say, "How would I know? Possibly to conserve power."

Ordinarily she would have gone no further, since his tone was even more than usually petulant, but she steeled herself and said, "Who are *they*, dear?"

"Who are who?" he snapped. "If you must talk, please try to be coherent, Martha."

"Who are *they* who might turn out the light when your eyes are closed?"

He sighed deeply and closed his book, leaving a forefinger at the page where he'd left off. He took off his pince-nez glasses and said, "I haven't the vaguest idea. But whoever they are, I am rapidly arriving at the opinion that they are managing this whole project extremely inefficiently. *Extremely* so."

She'd gone too far now to back down, so she said, as placatingly as possible, "What project, dear?"

He looked at her for a long moment, his mouth tight with impatience. "Very well," he said finally. "I see you intend to maintain the pretense to the end. Undoubtedly, those are your instructions.

"I give you to realize, and your superiors as well, that I have been aware of the true nature of—shall we say?—this *world*, for some time."

SHE BEGAN to open her mouth to say something but he flicked a hand at her negatively and went on. "The big mistake has been in making it so obviously fantastic. Whoever is in ultimate charge, might have been more successful in deceiving me had the sum total of your efforts added up to a bit more plausibility."

"But...Jeremiah..."

"Quiet please, until I finish, Martha. I have been aware for a considerable period that the sole reason for the existence of this so-called world and everyone in it, and all that goes on in it has been to keep the true nature of things from me; to befuddle my mind and so confuse me that I remain unaware of actuality. Very well, I contend that the undertaking is being poorly administered. I admit that I don't really understand *why* this is being done, but whatever the reason it is quite slipshod, I assure you. Quite."

He replaced his glasses on the bridge of his nose and went back to his book, obviously content to leave the subject at that point.

But Martha was inordinately valiant tonight. She said, "What is fantastic, Jeremiah? I don't believe I understand quite what—"

He sighed deeply once again, placed his book on the tea table before him and returned his glasses to his pocket.

"Almost everything," he said quietly. For a moment he looked as though he'd forgotten her, that he was talking to himself. His eyes went to the ceiling and he continued softly, "Almost all of it is utterly fantastic.

"Take, for instance, our governmental and social systems. Is there a sane one on earth?"

"You shouldn't speak against the government, dear," she said primly, evidently feeling fairly sure of herself on this point.

"The socio-economic system of this country is fantastic in the extreme," he said, ignoring her. "You would think it impossible that a more ridiculous one could exist; but all you have to do is look to England to find it. Of course, when you get to the Soviet Union things degenerate into absolute burlesque.

"But that isn't enough; where the whole project really becomes absurd to the point of extravaganza is the relationship between individuals. Take the relation between the sexes as the classic example. It would be difficult to imagine anything more utterly farcical than that two persons—such as you and I, for instance—should fall in love, whatever that is supposed to be, and remain in juxtaposition with each other for the balance of their lives. The supposed ultimate purpose of this, of course, is the breeding of further 'humans' to continue the insanity of it all."

Martha began crying.

"Please," he snapped. "I shall develop the point no further. I merely wished to make it clear that I *know*, that I realize it is all a farce and that you are part of the farce. You may continue playing your part…"

HE TOOK his glasses from his pocket, rearranged them carefully on his nose again and returned to the findings of Dr. Kinsey. "I am surprised that *they* allowed the printing of this book," he remarked in general.

After a lengthy period of sobbing to which he remained immune, Martha dried her eyes bravely and stammered, "Possibly you should see a doctor, dear."

Without looking up, her husband informed her, "I was expecting that suggestion momentarily. Please don't bother to mention it again."

"Yes, dear. But, Jeremiah—"

He put his book down for the third time and closed his eyes for a long moment. Finally he opened them and looked at her severely. "Martha," he said, "I consider myself a more than average tolerant person; however, I am becoming extremely weary of this conversation. I will repeat my conclusions once more, then I wish to hear no more about it.

"The question of whether or not the light remains on is comparatively unimportant although admittedly it has intrigued me. The important consideration is that I am aware of the nature of this so-called world and its inhabitants and I am not deceived."

He shifted around in his chair so that his back was to her and reached out for his book again.

"Very well," Martha said, "if you are not deceived, there is little reason to carryon the attempted deception."

"None at all," he muttered testily.

So Martha dissolved into her true shape and slithered across the living room floor and out the front door to report to her superiors.

Jeremiah Perkins didn't bother to look up as she left.

THE END

Navy Day

By HARRY HARRISON

The Army had a new theme song: "Anything you can do, we can do better!"
And they meant anything, including up-to-date hornpipes!

GENERAL WINGROVE looked at the rows of faces without seeing them. His vision went beyond the Congress of the United States, past the balmy June day to another day that was coming. A day when the Army would have its destined place of authority.

He drew a deep breath and delivered what was perhaps the shortest speech ever heard in the hallowed halls of Congress:

"The General Staff of the U.S. Army requests Congress to abolish the archaic branch of the armed forces known as the U.S. Navy."

The aging Senator from Georgia checked his hearing aid to see if it was in operating order, while the press box emptied itself in one concerted rush and a clatter of running feet that died off in the direction of the telephone room. A buzz of excited comment ran through the giant chamber. One by one the heads turned to face the Naval section where rows of blue figures stirred and buzzed like smoked-out bees. The knot of men around a paunchy figure heavy with gold braid broke up and Admiral Fitzjames climbed slowly to his feet.

Lesser men have quailed before that piercing stare, but General Wingrove was never the lesser man. The admiral tossed his head with disgust, every line of his body denoting outraged dignity. He turned to his audience, a small pulse beating in his forehead.

"I cannot comprehend the general's attitude, nor can I understand why he has attacked the Navy in this unwarranted fashion. The Navy has existed and will always exist as the first barrier of American defense. I ask you, gentlemen, to ignore this request as you would ignore the statements of any person...er, slightly demented. I should like to offer a recommendation that the general's sanity be investigated, and an inquiry be made as to the mental health of anyone else connected with this preposterous proposal!"

The general smiled calmly. "I understand, Admiral, and really don't blame you for being slightly annoyed. But, please let us not bring this issue of national importance down to a shallow personal level. The Army has facts to back up this request—facts that shall be demonstrated tomorrow morning."

Turning his back on the raging admiral, General Wingrove included all the assembled solons in one sweeping gesture.

"Reserve your judgment until that time, gentlemen, make no hasty judgments until you have seen the force of argument with which we back up our request. It is the end of an era. In the morning the Navy joins its fellow fossils, the dodo and the brontosaurus."

The admiral's blood pressure mounted to a new record and the gentle thud of his unconscious body striking the floor was the only sound to break the shocked silence of the giant hall.

THE EARLY morning sun warmed the white marble of the Jefferson Memorial and glinted from the soldiers' helmets and the roofs of the packed cars that crowded forward in a slow-moving stream. All the gentlemen of Congress were there, the passage of their cars cleared by the screaming sirens of motorcycle policemen. Around and under the wheels of the official cars pressed a solid wave of government workers and common citizens of the capital city. The trucks of the radio and television services pressed close, microphones and cameras extended.

The stage was set for a great day. Neat rows of olive drab vehicles curved along the water's edge. Jeeps and half-tracks shouldered close by weapons carriers and six-bys, all of them shrinking to insignificance beside the looming Patton tanks. A speakers' platform was set up in the center of the line, near the audience.

At precisely 10 a.m. General Wingrove stepped forward and scowled at the crowd until they settled into an uncomfortable silence. His speech was short and consisted of nothing more than amplifications of his opening statement that actions speak louder than words. He pointed to the first truck in line, a 2½-ton filled with an infantry squad sitting stiffly at attention.

The driver caught the signal and kicked the engine into life; with a grind of gears it moved forward toward the river's edge. There was an indrawn gasp from the crowd as the front wheels ground over the marble parapet—then the truck was plunging down towards the muddy waters of the Potomac.

The wheels touched the water and the surface seemed to sink while taking on a strange glassy character. The truck roared into high gear and rode forward on the surface of the water surrounded by a saucer-shaped depression. It parked two-hundred yards off shore and the soldiers, goaded by the sergeant's bark, leapt out and lined up with a showy *present arms*.

The general returned the salute and waved to the remaining vehicles. They moved forward in a series of maneuvers that indicated a great number of rehearsal hours on some hidden pond. The tanks rumbled slowly over the water while the jeeps cut back and forth through their lines in intricate patterns. The trucks backed and turned like puffing ballerinas.

The audience was rooted in a hushed silence, their eyeballs bulging. They continued to watch the amazing display as General Wingrove spoke again:

"You see before you a typical example of Army ingenuity, developed in Army laboratories. These motor units are supported on the surface of the water by an intensifying of the surface tension in their immediate area. Their weight is evenly distributed over the surface, causing the shallow depressions you see around them.

"This remarkable feat has been accomplished by the use of the *Dornifier*. A remarkable invention that is named after that brilliant scientist, Colonel Robert A. Dorn, Commander of the Brooke Point Experimental Laboratory. It was there that one of the civilian employees discovered the Dorn effect—under the Colonel's constant guidance, of course.

"Utilizing this invention the Army now becomes master of the sea as well as the land. Army convoys of trucks and tanks can blanket the world. The surface of the water is our highway, our motor park, our battleground—the airfield and runway for our planes."

Mechanics were pushing a Shooting Star onto the water. They stepped clear as flame gushed from the tail pipe; with the familiar whooshing rumble it sped down the Potomac and hurled itself into the air.

"When this cheap and simple method of crossing oceans is adopted it will of course mean the end of that fantastic medieval anachronism, the Navy. No need for billion-dollar aircraft carriers, battleships, dry-docks and all the other cumbersome junk that keeps those boats and things afloat. Give the taxpayer back his hard-earned dollar!"

Teeth grated in the Naval section as carriers and battleships were called "boats" and the rest of America's sea might lumped under the casual heading of "things." Lips were curled at the transparent appeal to the taxpayer's pocketbook. But with leaden hearts they knew that all this justified wrath and contempt would avail them nothing. This was Army Day with a vengeance, and the doom of the Navy seemed inescapable.

The Army had made elaborate plans for what they called "Operation Sinker." Even as the general spoke the publicity mills ground into high gear. From coast to coast the citizens absorbed the news with their morning nourishment.

"...Agnes, you hear what the radio said? The Army's gonna give a trip around the world in a B-36 as first prize in this limerick contest. All you have to do is fill in the last line, and mail one copy to the Pentagon and the other to the Navy..."

The Naval mail room had standing orders to burn all the limericks when they came in, but some of the newer men seemed to think the entire thing was a big joke. Commander Bullman found one in the mess hall:

The Army will always be there,
On the land, on the sea, in the air
So why should the Navy
Take all of the gravy...

to which a seagoing scribe had added:

And not give us ensigns our share?

The newspapers were filled daily with photographs of mighty B-36's landing on Lake Erie, and grinning soldiers making mock beachhead attacks on Coney Island. Each man wore a buzzing black box at his waist and walked on the bosom of the now quiet Atlantic like a biblical prophet.

Radio and television also carried the thousands of news releases that poured in an unending flow from the Pentagon Building. Cards, letters, telegrams and packages descended on Washington in an overwhelming torrent. The Navy Department was the unhappy recipient of deprecatory letters and a vast quantity of little cardboard battleships.

The people spoke and their representatives listened closely. This was an election year. There didn't seem to be much doubt as to the decision, particularly when the reduction in the budget was considered.

It took Congress only two months to make up its collective mind. The people were all pro-Army. The novelty of the idea had fired their imaginations.

They were about to take the final vote in the Lower House. If the amendment passed it would go to the states for ratification, and their votes were certain to follow that of Congress. The Navy had fought a last-ditch battle to no avail. The balloting was going to be pretty much of a sure thing—the wet water Navy would soon become ancient history.

For some reason the admirals didn't look as unhappy as they should.

THE NAVAL Department had requested one last opportunity to address the Congress. Congress had patronizingly granted permission, for even the doomed man is allowed one last speech. Admiral Fitzjames, who had recovered from his choleric attack, was the appointed speaker.

"Gentlemen of the Congress of the United States. We in the Navy have a fighting tradition. We 'damn the torpedoes' and sail straight ahead into the enemy's fire if that is necessary. We have been stabbed in the back—we have suffered a second Pearl Harbor sneak attack! The Army relinquished its rights to fair treatment with this attack. Therefore we are *counter-attacking!*" Worn out by his attacking and mixed metaphors, the Admiral mopped his brow.

"Our laboratories have been working night and day on the perfection of a device we hoped we would never be forced to use. It is now in operation, having passed the final trials a few days ago.

"The significance of this device *cannot* be underestimated. We are so positive of its importance that we are *demanding* that the *Army* be abolished!"

He waved his hand towards the window and bellowed one word.

"LOOK!"

Everyone looked. They blinked and looked again. They rubbed their eyes and kept looking.

Sailing majestically up the middle of Constitution Avenue was the battleship Missouri.

The Admiral's voice rang through the room like a trumpet of victory.

"The Mark-1 Debinder, as you see, temporarily lessens the binding energies that hold molecules of solid matter together. Solids become liquids, and a ship equipped with this device can sail anywhere in the world—on sea *or* land. Take your vote, gentlemen; the world awaits your decision."

THE END

The Survivors

By T. D. HAMM

Step by grueling step the four of them slogged their way toward a perilous safety. It was a magnificent display of the will for survival. The only question was, whose survival?

THERE were only four of them now. Soames and Rutherford had literally gone down with the ship in a roar of cascading rock and sand. Out of fifty square miles of the Martian plateau they had been unlucky enough to sit down on the eggshell thin roof of a sector honey-combed with caves. Scant moments after the exploring party had disembarked, Soames' comments on their resemblance to a Sunday School picnic were suddenly broken off by a cacophonous medley of yells, the rolling thunder of sliding rock, and over all the agonized metallic shrieking of tortured metal as the ship fell, crushed and twisted. There came a final tremendous roar as the fuel tanks blew. The ground heaved convulsively, and shuddered into silence.

Stunned and deafened, Bradford, Canham, Palmer and Rodriguez pulled themselves to their feet, staring dazedly at the towering column of dust hanging like a malevolent genie over the half-mile wide chasm.

Palmer, white with shock, lunged forward, turning indignantly as Bradford's arm jerked him back.

"Soames—and Rutherford—" he stuttered. "We've got to do something!"

Bradford's lip twisted mirthlessly.

"What're you going to do—jump in after them? If there was anything left of them the fuel tanks took care of it. They're gone—we're here. And we'd better start figuring out what we're going to do about it."

The four of them looked at each other silently. They knew as well as he, what they faced. Theirs had been the task of setting up a temporary exploring base till the supply ship arrived in three months—with luck.

Supplies for six months and all their equipment except their emergency rations had gone down with the ship. No hope there—might as well explore the Grand Canyon with a teaspoon as to try to salvage anything under that million tons of rock. Compressed food they had, two weeks supply per man; their extra oxygen tanks; an extra battery apiece for the suit heaters. Water would be their worst problem.

Bradford looked at the miles of barren, reddish wasteland and shrugged fatalistically.

"If there's any water at all, it will be at the Polar cap. We might as well get going—we've got a long hike."

Palmer grimaced wryly. "Forward, you Eagle Scouts. We can get our merit badges easy."

"Yeah, we can get them from Santa Claus at the Pole—" Rodriguez made a valiant attempt at his usual sardonic humor.

They piled a small cairn of the red rocks and Bradford planted the green and white flag of the Federated Nations. Encased in its protective covering he placed a note at its foot indicating their destination.

"We ought to sign it 'Kilroy,'" Canham grunted as they trudged forward. "Say, how far do we have to walk?'

"Around a hundred and fifty to two hundred miles."

Their concerted whistle of dismay echoing oddly in their ear-phones, they set out in thoughtful silence across the red face of Mars, the hovering dust blotting out their footprints as they went.

Three days and seventy-five miles later, they huddled wearily against the face of a small cliff shivering in the icy chill of the night wind. They had found a desiccated bush or two in a protected nook during the afternoon and carried it with them.

Now, they fed the wiry twigs into the fire with miserly care glad of its meager light against the haunted dark.

Rodriguez held a branch to the firelight. "Looks like a sort of poorhouse cousin to birch," he hazarded. "Wonder if they ever had forests on this God-forgotten planet?"

Palmer grinned. "Well, at least there is still life of sorts. Rutherford would have flipped his lid over those comical little fellows we saw today."

A half dozen times they had seen furry little marsupials, downy as chinchillas, their young poking out inquisitive snouts toward the interlopers and as promptly getting them slapped down again.

A flicker of motion on the perimeter of firelight caught his eye. "We've got a visitor," he whispered. "There's one of the little beggars now."

He tossed a crumb from his plate toward the peering head. Flicking a tongue like a lizard's, the visitor fielded it neatly in midair and advanced, peering hopefully at the circle of grinning faces. Palmer stretched out a stealthy hand and gripped it gently about the middle as it sniffed at his food can.

"Look at him," he cried delightedly. "He doesn't even squirm. He likes me!"

He tickled its ears, sliding his fingers down through the heavy, silky pelt. "You could make a fortune with these..." he dropped it abruptly with an anguished yelp and a string of blistering oaths, while his friends clung to each other and howled mirthfully.

"Your little friend, he pulled a knife on you. No?" queried Rodriguez sympathetically. The grin faded from his suddenly startled face.

"Amigo, que lo es? Hey, fellows—something's wrong!"

Palmer, his face shocked and dazed had dropped to his knees, whimpering and retching painfully.

"My God, look—his hand," whispered Bradford.

They had removed their bulky gloves before eating and Palmers exposed hand was black and swollen beyond recognition. Even as they watched, the skin split, leaking watery fluid. His body contorted, he rolled on the ground screaming with unbearable agony.

Bradford's hand dropped to his pistol and fell away again. He looked at the others pleadingly.

"We can't let him suffer this way. But my God—I *can't* do it..."

Canham looked at him dully. "You won't have to—he's finished."

The rigidly contorted body relaxed inertly, the tortured eyes open and glazed. Rodriguez crossed himself and burst into childish sobs.

Bradford put out a restraining hand toward Canham.

"Let him alone—I wish to God I could do the same thing. Give me a hand with Palmer—we'll have to bury him the best way we can."

Shaken with more than the night chill, they removed the clumsy oxygen and water containers and piled a protective cairn of rocks above the silent figure. Behind them, Rodriguez sobbed bitter Spanish curses and hurled rocks at telltale flickers of movement in the dark.

Through the next day and the next, they trudged on doggedly, speaking little as they put the reluctant miles behind them, taking what shelter they could during the bitter nights. During the day under the thin Martian sunlight, they turned off the suit-heaters, conserving the batteries; hoarding their remaining food and water with miserly care.

Bradford, assuming tacitly acknowledged leadership, pondered the situation wearily. Even with Palmer's supplies, it was doubtful that the three of them could last out the ten weeks or so remaining before the arrival of the second ship. If they could only make it to the Pole—there they were sure of water at least, in the vegetation belt surrounding the shallow icecap. If it was ice and not frozen carbon dioxide, which some of the experts held out for. In their initial swing around the planet they had seen the narrow green belt dotted with shining pools. Plants meant oxygen, too; and it was possible that in a temperature supporting some kind of growing life, it would be warm enough so that they could remove their helmets for breathing, if only in the brief daylight hours.

Bradford, lost in thought, started as Canham touched his arm, motioning him to open his faceplate and turn off the headphones.

"What's the matter with you?" he jerked impatiently.

Canham turned a thumb toward Rodriguez.

"Nothing's the matter with me. Him—I think he's going off his rocker."

Bradford looked at Rodriguez plodding unheedingly ahead. Since his first outburst after Palmer's death, he had gone mechanically about each day's routine, outwardly calm. He said little, but neither had the others. The only indication of his inner torment was when one of the deadly little marsupials peered at them as they went on their way. With deadly fury, he would hurl a barrage of rocks through the air, while the little animal eyed them in indifferent curiosity. Occasionally he scored a hit, laughing grimly as the dying animal erected the ruff of lethal spines through its silky fur.

Bradford snorted mirthlessly. "I doubt if either of us would pass a sanity test at the moment," he grunted. "What's so special about him?"

Canham's normally cheerful face retained its solemn worry.

"I know what you mean—but, watch him next time one of those dust devils comes by."

The day before they had descended the northern slope of the high plateau onto the long, sandy plain that extended northward. Everywhere there were the dancing, careening dust devils, tall columns of the brick-red sand; faintly menacing forms pursuing some unseen purpose of their own. From time to time, one would swerve close, seeming to keep pace with them for a few steps before whirling off ill its erratic dance.

One approached them now. Rodriguez turned toward it making a furtive gesture with thumb and forefinger and deliberately trickled a stream from his water bottle upon the sand.

Bradford came forward on the run, shouting into the hastily adjusted helmet mike. Angrily he jerked the bottle out of Rodriguez' unresisting hand.

"What the hell do you think you're playing at?" Bradford panted.

Rodriguez eyed him sullenly.

"I know these things, as my people know them. *Los Bailerines del Diablo*—the devil dancers. One gives them what is most precious. *Es muy necessario.*" More and more he was losing his usually fluent, faintly accented English and reverting to his native tongue.

Bradford eyed him sternly.

"Rodriguez, you are a good Catholic. You wear a holy medal. What's all this talk about sacrifices to the devil?"

Rodriguez' gaze slid away. "I don't think God knows about this place. This is of *El Diablo.*"

"So now you want to get in good with the Devil," Bradford grunted. "Well, you can do it some other way than with the last of the water." He jerked his head at Canham waiting wearily behind them.

"Come on, you two. We'll all feel better when we get out of this—desert." He ended with a wry twist of the lips. He had nearly said 'god-forsaken.' Maybe Rodriguez had the right idea after all.

During the afternoon, some chance convection of air currents sharply increased the dust whirls. The desert seemed full of their erratic, spinning shapes. Rodriguez plodded along, ignoring Canham's sporadic attempts at conversation. The chilly sunlight was waning and Bradford's face lighted with relief at the sight of a small sand hill. At least they could dig a hole to get their backs into and break the whistling winds. He felt an irrational comfort at the thought of the coming darkness—at least they wouldn't be able to see the dust devils. Maybe they could get some talk going and snap Rodriguez out of his melancholy silence. Perhaps they had all been getting too introverted since the series of disasters.

They made camp before dark, digging themselves well in; Bradford and Canham forced themselves into a semblance of cheerfulness as they worked. Rodriguez' face remained dark and unsmiling. Like one of those damned stone images in the Yucatan jungle, Bradford thought with a brief burst of irritation. You wouldn't think that the little Mexican had been the ship's humorist, his face one perpetual white-toothed smile.

As they huddled cold and uncomfortable in the gathering darkness, Canham grinned apologetically and with the air of a conjuror producing trained seals from a hat, gravely presented three crushed and bent but undeniable cigarettes, distinctly contraband on the ship. He eyed Bradford with mock contrition.

"I can't imagine how I got these in my kit. I guess when I was packing everything just went black. Of course, if you'd care to be my companion in crime…?"

Bradford frowned darkly. "I ought to have you in irons for this, Mr. Canham! Now give me one of those things before I break your arm!"

With a muttered word of thanks, Rodriguez laid his carefully aside on a handy rock and slid out of the shelter into the early dark. Canham tossed a facetious remark after him and received the usual unprintable reply.

The other two sat, inhaling luxuriously. Bradford sighed comfortably.

"I think he's snapping out of it. Good thing you noticed what was happening. We'll all have to keep an eye on each other from now on."

"It's enough to drive anybody nuts. Have you noticed anything funny about—well, about the *feel* of the place?"

Bradford looked at him uneasily.

"What do you mean 'funny'?"

"It's just a feeling I get; you know how a brand-new house that's never been lived in feels different than an old house that's been deserted? They're both empty, but it's a different emptiness. It's the same way with pieces of country—where we trained on that high desert country in Arizona, it had a new, sort of *unused* feeling about it."

Bradford felt an unacknowledged tingling along his nerve ends.

"Well, this is a lot *like* it—" he tossed out defensively. In spite of himself he slid a sidelong glance at the surrounding dark.

Canham went on unnoticing.

"That's what I mean—it's a lot like it, but it's different too. Like it had been lived in for God knows how long, but everybody moved out."

"But there's no ruins, or anything—"

"Maybe there wouldn't be any after a million years or so. And how do we know what's under the sand? You can't even find your own footprints fifteen minutes after you've made them."

Bradford laughed shortly. "Well, keep your spooky ideas to yourself. We don't want Rodriguez going clear off his rocker."

They sat watching the fading landscape where the dust devils still swooped and swung. Finally, with a faint frown, Bradford glanced at his chronometer.

"Roddy's been gone quite a while," he said uneasily. He stood suddenly and lifted his voice sharply.

"Rodriguez! Hey, amigo—andale Ud.!" He glanced at Canham. "I don't like this—we don't know what we're liable to run onto in this damned country..."

They set out, trotting clumsily in their heavy suits, circling the mound where Rodriguez' footprints were already fading in the shifting sands, Canham gave a sudden convulsive clutch at his companion's arm. There was no need to speak—scattered over the sand were the component parts of a space suit; the heavy gloves, the helmet, the shoes. And neatly wrapped in the padded coverall the oxygen tanks. Ahead, nearly invisible, were the prints of naked feet.

Bradford groaned. "Good God, he's gone completely nuts. He'll be frozen stiff in ten minutes!"

They saw the crumpled heap at the same moment and with a thrill of indefinable terror they saw the stooping, whirling shadow, spinning dizzily over the huddled shape.

Bradford wrenched his faceplate open, yelling frantically. Gasping, he slammed the mask shut against something like a rain of fiery sparks on his unprotected skin. It was all too evident that Rodriguez would never hear again.

Gathering his strength to turn the inert figure, he nearly overbalanced—there was no weight to it at all. Beside him, Canham cried out hoarsely, "My God…he's like a…like a mummy!"

The whole figure looked strangely unhuman. Completely dehydrated, the flesh molded tight over the protruding bones. Rodriguez lay peacefully, both stick-like hands clasped over the holy medal on his chest.

Sick and shaken, they bent to the task of scooping sand over the shrunken body, glancing sidelong at the devil-dancers whirling exultantly in the shadowy night.

Bradford with a defiant look at his companion, unhooked Rodriguez' half-empty water bottle from his own belt and placed it upright at the head of the mound.

"He knew what they wanted and I took it away from him. I guess we can spare him this."

Retrieving the oxygen tank and the heat batteries as they went, they trudged wearily back to their meager shelter, sickeningly conscious of the vacant space beside them.

Canham gave a sudden choked exclamation.

"He didn't even get to smoke his cigarette—"

Bradford caught his up-thrown arm. "He left it for us. When things get tough we'll share it."

Canham gave an hysterical giggle. "When 'things get tough'—! Goodnight, Hardrock!"

The two days following went by in a continuous waking nightmare—putting one foot in front of the other foot, inching their way monotonously toward the still invisible Pole. They had left the dust devils behind—due to some freakishness of the wind, so they figured.

Canham looks like Death on a pale horse, Bradford thought dully. And I probably look worse. He rubbed absently at the dry, scaly pits on his face where the unholy dust had stung him and reverted to his private worry. Suppose the carefully theorized solar compass was wrong? Suppose this double-damned planet possessed a field of its own that would throw their calculations out and they were going in circles? If they were heading North, the Pole couldn't be more than another day or two distant even if his reckoning had been off.

Unconsciously he lengthened his stride for a few paces, and was reminded by his quickened breathing that he was wasting his scant oxygen supply. They already had tapped their original spare tanks, thankful for the lessened weight as they jettisoned the empty. Even with Palmer and Rodriguez' partly filled tanks they only had enough for a couple of days full time use. Since they had left the region of the whirlwinds, they had been able to experiment cautiously with leaving their faceplates open a few minutes at a time, even though the thin, oxygen-starved air caused their lungs to labor painfully.

Bradford was roused from his musings by an astonished exclamation from his companion. Down on his knees, Canham was babbling incoherently, "—green! It's green!"

Bradford knelt beside him in awestruck silence. A tiny growth scarcely large enough to be dignified with the title of shrub, here in this arid plain and undeniably—green! Canham touched it caressingly.

"Baby, I hope all your brothers and sister and the rest of the kinfolk are just over the hill."

Clambering to their feet, they set off, lumbering awkwardly in their heavy suits, breath coming in labored gasps to halt abruptly at the edge of a steep downward slope. Before them lay another belt of arid sand and beyond a ring of marshy, pool-dotted soil encircling a solid belt of vivid green—and faintly visible on the horizon, the glimmer of the shallow snowcap.

Canham gulped audibly. "If Cortez really wanted a thrill, he should have discovered this overgrown duck pond. The Pacific—phooey!"

Bradford slapped him on the back. "I feel like I could flap my wings and *fly* down. Last one in's a rotten egg…"

Laughing with almost hysterical relief, they ran, waddled and slid, heedless of bumps and oxygen wastage. They picked themselves up at the bottom, grinning sheepishly.

"If Space Authority could only see us now," Canham chortled. "Let us now with due dignity take possession of our kingdom."

Jubilantly they strode ahead, bowing to imaginary cheering crowds.

"We've got it made, Hardrock. We got it made!"

Bradford's grin wavered. "Well…we've got it made this far anyway, with two months and half to go. Let's hope there's duck on that pond…"

Suddenly sobered they went on; before them the semi-arid belt seemed to stretch interminably toward the barely visible green area. The horizon seemed to retreat as they advanced.

"Another night in this damned desert," Bradford groaned. "At least we may be able to get a fire going with this brush—and a real swallow of water apiece. I hope that stuff we saw out there wasn't a mirage," he added disconsolately.

"Not that—that was real honest-to-God water. Wish I'd brought my duck gun. These damn supply sergeants never do send out the right equipment."

Towards dusk they scooped out a shallow hole in the sand and roofed it with green branches.

"With our luck this stuff will probably turn out to be poison ivy," Canham predicted gloomily. "Join me in my thatched hut, oh beauteous one—and look out for sandburrs."

They slept fitfully, shivering through the long night hours. Bradford announced that this was undoubtedly the North Pole and they had arrived at the beginning of the six months night. With the first of the thin, cheerless rays of the distant sun, they clambered out of their cramped sleeping place, some of yesterday's enthusiasm waning as they stumbled about, relaxing stiffened muscles.

Vaguely uneasy and depressed they started out; the very nearness of their goal somehow seemed to make their chances of reaching it doubly unsure.

Afternoon brought them to the edge of the marshy area; they halted, surveying it doubtfully. Any such region on Earth would have been busy with life—frogs croaking on lily pads, water rats and fish making small plopping sounds in the water, tall reeds swaying. Here there was nothing that breathed of warm-blooded life. Only the shallow pools lying stagnant, reflecting stubby water-grasses, dotted here and there with small mounds growing a stunted bush or two.

Canham shivered suddenly. "This is more dead than a cypress swamp. How I'd love to see a little old cottonmouth rearing his ugly head out of that puddle."

Bradford shifted his shoulders uneasily.

"Well, here goes. Shall we circle around a bit to see if there's a dryer path?"

An hour's walking brought no change; always before them lay the silent marsh, inimical in its unending desolation. And beyond it, tantalizingly green, lay the only growing things on Mars.

With some difficulty they managed to find a branch apiece long enough for a probing pole and started out reluctantly, wincing as their feet sank deep in the fetid ooze.

"These boots are damned heavy," Bradford remarked doubtfully.

"You take yours off if you want to," Canham returned emphatically. "I'm damned if I'm going to step on some slimy, poisonous species of fauna in my bare feet."

They forged ahead doggedly, tapping with their poles, making for a stunted shrub lifting itself above the rest. Bradford, slightly in the lead, whirled as Canham gave a stifled yelp and hauled himself up on the mound, looking slightly green.

"Felt like a whale turned under my foot," he panted. "Let's get out of this so I can be sick—"

Foot by foot, they heaved and plunged their way through the relentless sucking mire.

"We must be nearly to the other side," Bradford wheezed. "We've got to make it before dark. It's a cinch we can't camp here."

Canham looked across the few hundred yards remaining and shook his head wearily.

"This thing is like a moat; I get the feeling that we're being kept out by one defense after another. Those harmless looking, poisonous little beasts that killed Palmer, the wind devils that got Rodriguez and now—this."

Bradford repressed a shiver. "Come on," he said roughly. "Don't start telling your ghost stories here, for the love of heaven. Save them for your kids."

They plopped off the further side of the mound, their feet making gobbling noises as they lifted them one after the other in the tenacious, clinging mud. Bradford halted suddenly.

"There it is," he breathed. "You can see the shore from here…"

Caution forgotten, they plunged ahead, panting with effort. Canham gave a sudden startled cry.

"Brad! I can't—lift—my foot! I can't move it!"

Bradford, a few steps to the right, felt his heart leap sickeningly at the stark terror in the voice.

"Take it easy! Get a grip on my pole—*now!*"

He heaved strongly, feet slipping, unable to get a purchase to make his strength felt against the pull of the quicksand. The perspiration trickled into his smarting eyes. Through Canham's faceplate, he could see his face set in agonized strain as he attempted to free his feet in their heavy boots, the water level rising from waist to armpits as he struggled. Bradford redoubled his efforts, muscles cracking as he tried to heave the other free bodily. Canham relaxed suddenly.

"It's no use," he panted heavily. "Don't come closer—it'll just get both of us. Don't stay and watch it it'll just make it harder. Wait a minute—here, catch!"

With a last convulsive effort, he jerked loose the oxygen tank and gave it a desperate throw. Bradford automatically caught it, nearly going off-balance and righting himself with panic-stricken effort.

"Hold on! Hold on—" he gritted. "I'll get some branches from that shrub; you can throw yourself forward so I can get a grip on you."

Canham looked at him palely.

"No use. But, I'm not going under with my helmet on, still alive, under—*this!*"

He shuddered queasily, and with one quick jerk freed his faceplate as he went under. For a moment the water boiled furiously as the remaining oxygen in his suit released. Then Bradford stood alone, staring stupidly with shock, watching as the bubbles rose more and more slowly and died away.

He had no recollection of floundering the remaining hundred yards to the shore. Physically sick and shaking with horror, he ploughed through the shallowing ooze and fell headlong on wet, but solid earth.

The sun was sinking as he finally stirred, groaning, and pulled himself further away from the haunted ooze. Incredibly, he slept at last, waking to the first rays of the sun, dazed and unbelieving. Turning instinctively for the reassurance of another face, remembrance hit him like a plow. Bile came up into his mouth as he wrenched his faceplate open and was grindingly, shudderingly sick.

The spasm over, he heaved himself to his feet, staring about stupidly. Surely there was something he had to do? Every morning for so long he had had to lift himself to his feet and force himself to go on till dark—toward the Pole.

But—here *was* the green and a few miles away the hoarfrost glitter of the snowcap. There was nowhere to go!

"We made it—" he said uncertainly, looking around. But there was no one to share the triumph. Dully, he thought of them all—Palmer, betrayed by a gentle, kitten-like thing—Rodriguez, a human sacrifice to something utterly alien—Canham, dead on the edge of victory. He looked at Canham's oxygen canister and laid his hand on it gently. Then slowly, with dragging steps, he went on toward the shining green that had cost them so much to achieve.

The ground and the air above it as he approached were strangely warm. And the plants too, were warm and oddly different. No biologist, he dimly sensed a difference from any growth that Earth knew. The stems, the leaves were veined with pulsing red and at the tip of each stem, a flower lifted, shaped like an open mouth. There was a space between each plant, none crowded his neighbor. It was very orderly and pleasant and so warm—so warm. He opened his faceplate.

Drowsy and relaxed, no longer driven by unrelenting urgency, he found himself nodding dreamily as he walked between the tall stems. With a sigh of pleasure he laid down among them, conscious of the verge of sleep of an insistent demanding whisper—"More air! Give us air!" Unhesitatingly, he opened the gauge of the oxygen tank, drifting into a sea of darkness.

The red-veined plants about him pulsed with a quicker rhythm as the thousand opened mouths drank in the air, rich with a richness they had not known for a million years. And about the unconscious form of the man, poured the carbon dioxide from the lips of a thousand oxygen breathing creatures.

They had had a million years to learn the technique of survival as the atmosphere of their planet drained off into space. Retreating, adapting, eon by eon to their last stronghold; ringed round by their guardians of the Earth, the Air and the Water.

Here were the Survivors.

THE END

Cocoon

By KEITH LAUMER

Two billion years ago, a unit of life had the urge to climb out of the sea. It died. But that didn't count. The urge to climb out was the thing—greater in its force than a million suns. To keep that urge is the measure of a man.

SID Throndyke overrode his respirator to heave a deep sigh.

"Wow!" he said, flipping to his wife's personal channel. "A tough day on the Office channel."

The contact screens attached to his eyeballs stayed blank: Cluster was out. Impatiently, Sid toed the console, checking the channels: Light, Medium, and Deep Sitcom; auto-hypno; Light and Deep Narco; four, six and eight-party Social; and finally, muttering to himself, Psychan. Cluster's identity symbol appeared on his screens.

"There you are," he grieved. "Psychan again. After a hard day, the least a man expects is to find his wife tuned to his channel—"

"Oh, Sid; there's this wonderful analyst. A new model. It's doing so much for me, really wonderful..."

"I know," Sid grumped. "That orgasm-association technique. That's all I hear. I'd think you'd want to keep in touch with the Sitcoms, so you know what's going on; but I suppose you've been tied into Psychan all day—while I burned my skull out on Office."

"Now, Sid; didn't I program your dinner and everything?"

"Um." Mollified, Sid groped with his tongue for the dinner lever, eased the limp plastic tube into his mouth. He sucked a mouthful of the soft paste—

"Cluster! You know I hate Vege-pap. Looks like you could at least dial a nice Prote-sim or a Sucromash..."

"Sid, you ought to tune to Psychan. It would do you a world of good..." Her sub-vocalized voice trailed off in the earphones. Sid snorted, dialed a double Prote-sim AND a Sucromash, fuming at the delay. He gulped his dinner, not even noticing the rich gluey consistency, then in a somewhat better mood, flipped to the Light Sitcom.

It was good enough stuff, he conceded; the husband was a congenital psychopathic inferior who maintained his family in luxury by a series of fantastic accidents. You had to chuckle when his suicide attempt failed at the last moment, after he'd lost all that blood. The look on his face when they dragged him back...

But somehow it wasn't enough. Sid dialed the medium; it wasn't much better. The deep, maybe.

SID viewed for a few minutes with growing impatience. Sure, you had to hand it to the Sitcom people; there was a lot of meat in the deep sitcom. It was pretty subtle stuff, the way the wife got the money the husband had been saving and spent it for a vacation trip for her chihuahua; had a real social content, too deep for most folks. But like the rest of the sitcoms, it was historical. Sure, using old-time settings gave a lot of scope for action. But how about something more pertinent to the contemporary situation? Nowadays, even though people led the kind of rich, full lives that Vital Programming supplied, there was still a certain lack. Maybe it was just a sort of atavistic need for gross muscular exertion. He'd viewed a discussion of the idea of a few nights earlier on the usual Wednesday night four-party hookup with the boys. Still, in his case, he had plenty of muscle tone. He'd spent plenty on a micro-spasm attachment for use with the narco channel...

That was a thought. Sid didn't usually like narco; too synthetic, as he'd explained to the boys. They hadn't liked the remark, he remembered. Probably they were all narco fans. But what the hell, a man had a right to a few maverick notions.

Sid tuned to the Narco channel. It was a traditional sex fantasy, in which the familiar colorless hero repeatedly fended off the advances of coitus-seeking girls. It was beautifully staged, with plenty of action, but like the sitcoms, laid in one of those never-never historical settings. Sid flipped past with a sub-vocal grunt. It wasn't much better than Cluster's orgasm-association treatments.

The stylized identity-symbol of the Pubinf announcer flashed on Sid's screens, vibrating in resonance with the impersonal voice of the Official announcer:

"…cause for concern. CentProg states that control will have been re-established within the hour. Some discomfort may result from vibration in sectors north of Civic Center, but normalcy will be restored shortly. Now, a word on the food situation."

A hearty, gelatinous voice took over: "Say, folks, have you considered switching to Vege-pap? Vege-pap now comes in a variety of rich flavors, all, of course, equally nourishing, every big swallow loaded with the kind of molecule that keeps those metabolisms rocking along at the pace of today's more-fun-than-ever sitcoms—and today's stimulating narco and social channels, too!

"Starting with First Feeding tomorrow, you'll have that opportunity you've wanted to try Vege-pap. Old-fashioned foods, like Prote-sim and Sucromash, will continue to be available, of course, where exceptional situations warrant. Now—"

"What's that?" Sid sub-vocalized. He toed the replay key, listened again. Then he dug a toe viciously against the tuning key, flipping to the Psychan monitor.

CLUSTER!" he barked at his wife's identity pattern. "Have you heard about this nonsense? Some damn fool on Pubinf is blathering about Vege-pap for everybody! By God, this is a free country. I'd like to see anyone try—"

"Sid," Cluster's voice came faintly, imploring. "P-P-Please, S-S-Sid…"

"Damn it, Cluster…" Sid stopped talking, coughed, gulped. His throat was burning. In his excitement he'd been vocalizing. The realization steadied him. He'd have to calm down. He'd been behaving like an animal…

"Cluster, darling. Kindly interrupt your treatment. I have to talk to you. Now. It's important." Confound it, if she didn't switch to his channel now—

"Yes, Sid." Cluster's voice had a ragged undertone. Sid half-suspected she was vocalizing then too…

"I was listening to Pubinf," he said, aware of a sense of dignity in the telling. No narco-addict he, but a mature-minded auditor of a serious channel like Pubinf. "They're raving about cutting off Prote-sim. Never heard of such nonsense. Have you heard anything about this?"

"No, Sid. You should know I never—"

"I know! But I thought maybe you'd heard something…"

"Sid, I've been under treatment all day—except the time I spent programming your dinner."

"You can get Prote-sim in exceptional situations, they said! I wonder what that's supposed to mean? Why, I've been a Prote-sim man for years…"

"Maybe it will do you good, Sid. Something different…"

"Different? What in the world do I want with something different? I have a comfortable routine, well-balanced, creative. I'm not interested in having any government fat-head telling me what to eat."

"But Vege-pap might be good; build you up or something."

"Build me up? What are you talking about? I view sports regularly; and aren't you forgetting my Micro-spasm accessory? Hah! I'm a very physically-minded man, when it comes to that."

"I know you are, Sid. I didn't mean…I only meant, maybe a little variety…"

Sid was silent, thinking. Variety. Hmm. Might be something in that. Maybe he WAS in a rut, a little.

"Cluster," he said suddenly. "You know, it's a funny thing; I've kind of gotten out of touch. Oh, I don't mean with important affairs. Heck, I hardly ever tune in Narco, or auto-hypno, for that matter. But I mean, after all, it's been quite a while now I guess, since we gave up well, you know, physical contact."

"Sid! If you're going to be awful, I'm switching right back to my Psychan—"

"I don't mean to be getting personal, Cluster. I was just thinking... By golly, how long has it been since that first contract with CentProg?"

"Why—I haven't any idea. That was so long ago, I can't see what difference it makes. Heavens, Sid, life today is so rich and full—"

"Don't get me wrong, I'm not talking about wanting to change, or anything idiotic. Just wondering. You know."

"Poor Sid. If you could spend more time with wonderful channels like Psychan, and not have to bother with that boring old Office..."

SID chuckled sub-vocally. "A man needs the feeling of achievement he gets from doing a job, Cluster. I wouldn't be happy, just relaxing with Sitcom all the time. And after all, Indexing is an important job. If we fellows in the game all quit, where'd CentProg be? Eh?"

"I hadn't thought of it like that, Sid. I guess it is pretty important."

"Darn right kid. They haven't built the computer yet that can handle Indexing—or Value Judgment, or Criticism— It'll be a while yet before the machine replaces man." Sid chuckled again. Cluster was such a kid in a lot of ways.

Still, it had been a long time. Funny, how you didn't think much about time, under Vital Programming. After all, your program was so full, you didn't have time to moon over the past. You popped out of Dream-stim, had a fast breakfast (Vege-pap; hah! He'd see about that!), then over to Office channel. That kept a fellow on his toes, right up till quitting time. Then dinner with Cluster, and right into the evening's round of Sitcoms, Socials, Narcos—whatever you wanted.

But how long had it been? A long time, no doubt. Measured in, say, years, the way folks used to be in the habit of thinking.

Years and years. Yes, by golly. Years and years.

Quite suddenly, Sid was uneasy. How long had it been? He had been about twenty-eight—the term came awkwardly to mind—twenty-eight when he and Cluster first met. Then there was that first anniversary—a wild time that had been, with friends over for TV. And then Vital Programming had come along. He and Cluster had been among the first to sign up.

God, what a long time it had been. TV. Imagine sitting. The thought of being propped up against coarse chairs, out in the open, made Sid wince. And other people around—faces right out in the open and everything. Staring at a little screen no more than five feet square. How in the world had people stood it? Still, it was all in what you were used to. People were adaptable. They had had to be to survive in those primitive conditions. You had to give the old-timers credit. He and Cluster were a pretty lucky couple to have lived in the era when Vital Programming was developed. They could see the contrast right in their own lives. The younger folks, now—

"Sid," Cluster broke in plaintively. "May I finish my treatment now?"

Sid dialed off, annoyed. Cluster wasn't interested in his problems. She was so wrapped up in Psychan these days, she couldn't even discuss the sitcoms intelligently. Well, Sid Throndyke wasn't a man to be pushed around. He nudged the 'fone switch, gave a number. An operator answered.

"I want the Pubinf office."

THERE was a moment's silence. "That number is unavailable," the recorded voice said.

"Unavailable, hell! I want to talk to them down there! What's all this about cutting off Prote-sim?"

"That information is not available."

"Look," Sid said, calming himself with an effort. "I want to talk to someone at Pubinf—"

"The line is available now." An unfamiliar identity pattern appeared on Sid's screens.

"I want to find out about this food business," Sid began—

"A temporary measure," a harassed voice said. "Due to the emergency."

"What emergency?" Sid stared at the pattern belligerently. As he watched, it wavered, almost imperceptibly. A moment later, he felt a distinct tremor through the form-hugging plastic cocoon.

"What…" he gasped, "what was *that?*"

"There's no cause for alarm," the Pubinf voice said. "You'll be kept fully informed through regular—"

A second shock rumbled. Sid gasped. "What the devil's going on…?"

The Pubinf pattern was gone. Sid blinked at the blank screens, then switched to his monitor channel. He had to talk to someone. Cluster would be furious at another interruption, but—

"Sid!" Cluster's voice rasped in Sid's hemispherical canals. She was vocalizing now for sure, he thought wildly.

"They broke right in!" Cluster cried. "Just as I was ready to climax—"

"Who?" Sid demanded. "What's going on here? What are you raving about?"

"Not an identity pattern, either," Cluster wailed. "Sid, it was a—a—face."

"Wha—" Sid blinked. He hadn't heard Cluster use obscenity before. This must be serious.

"Calm yourself," he said. "Now tell me exactly what happened."

"I told you: a—face. It was horrible, Sid. O n the Psychan channel. And he was shouting—"

"Shouting what?"

"I don't know. Something about 'Get out.' Oh, Sid, I've never been so humiliated…"

"Listen, Cluster," Sid said. "You tune in to a nice narco now, and get some rest. I'll deal with this."

"A face," Cluster sobbed. "A great, nasty, *hairy* face—"

"That's *enough*," Sid snapped.

He cut Cluster's identity pattern with an impatient gouge of his toe. Sometimes it seemed like women enjoyed obscenity.

NOW what? He was far from giving up on the Vege-pap issue, and now this: a respectable married woman insulted right in her own cocoon. Things were going to hell. But he'd soon see about that. With a decisive twist of the ankle, Sid flipped to the Police channel.

"I want to report an outrage."

The police identity pattern blanked abruptly. For a moment Sid's contact screens were blank. Then a face appeared.

Sid sucked in a breath out of phase with his respirator. THIS wasn't the police channel. The face stared at him, mouth working: a pale face, with whiskers sprouting from hollow cheeks, lips sunken over toothless gums. Then the audio came in, in midsentence:

"…to warn you. You've got to listen, you fools! You'll all die here! It's already at the north edge of the city. The big barrier wall's holding, but—"

The screen blanked; the bland police pattern reappeared.

"The foregoing interruption was the result of circumstances beyond the control of CentProg," a taped voice said smoothly. "Normal service will now be resumed."

"Police!" Sid yelled. He was vocalizing now, and be damned to it! There was just so much a decent citizen would stand for—

The screen flickered again. The police pattern disappeared. Sid held his breath—

A face appeared. This was a different one, Sid was sure. It was hairier than the other one, but not as hollow-cheeked. He watched in dumb shock as the mouth opened—

"Listen," a hoarse voice said. "Everybody, listen. We're blanketing all the channels this time—I hope. This is our last try. There's only a few of us. It wasn't easy getting into here—and there's no time left. We've get to move fast."

The voice stopped as the man on the screen breathed hoarsely, swallowed. Then he went on:

"It's the ice; it's moving down on us, fast, a god-awful big glacier. The walls can't stand much longer. It'll either wipe the city off the map or bury it. Either way, anybody that stays is done for.

"Listen; it won't be easy, but you've got to try. Don't try to go down. You can't get out below because of the drifts. Go up, onto the roofs. It's your only chance—you must go up."

THE image on Sid's contact screens trembled violently, then blanked. Moments later, Sid felt a tremor—worse, this time. His cocoon seemed to pull at him. For a moment he was aware of the drag of a hundred tiny contacts grafted to the skin, a hundred tiny conductors penetrating to nerve conduits—

An almost suffocating wave of claustrophobia swept over him. The universe seemed to be crushing in on him, immobile, helpless, a grub buried in an immense anthill—

The shock passed. Slowly, Sid regained a grip on himself. His respirator was cycling erratically, attempting to match to his ragged breathing impulses. His chest ached from the strain. He groped with a toe, keyed in Cluster's identity pattern.

"Cluster! Did you feel it? Everything was rocking…"

There was no reply. Sid called again. No answer. Was she ignoring him, or—

Maybe she was hurt, alone and helpless—

Sid fought for calm. No need for panic. Dial CentProg, report the malfunction. He felt with trembling toes, and punched the keys…

CentProg's channel was dark, lifeless. Sid stared, unbelieving. It wasn't possible. He switched wildly to the light sitcom—

Everything normal here. The husband fell down the stairs, smashing his new camera…

But this was no time to get involved. Sid flipped through the medium and deep Sitcoms: all normal. Maybe he could get through to the police now—

Mel Goldfarb's pattern blinked on the personal call code. Sid tuned him in.

"Mel! What's it all about? My God, that earthquake—"

"I don't like it, Sid. I felt it, over here in South Sector. The…uh…face…said the North Sector. You're over that side. What did you—"

"My God, I thought the roof was going to fall in, Mel. It was terrible! Look, I'm trying to get through to the police. Keep in touch, hey?"

"Wait, Sid; I'm worried—"

Sid cut the switch, flipped to the police channel. If that depraved son of a bitch showed his face again—

The police pattern appeared. Sid paused to gather his thoughts. First things first…

"That earthquake," he said. "What's happening? And the maniac who's been exposing his face. My wife—"

"The foregoing interruption was the result of circumstances beyond the control of CentProg. Normal service will now be resumed."

"What are you talking about? NOTHING is beyond the control of CentProg—"

"The foregoing interruption was the result of circumstances beyond the control of CentProg. Normal service will now be resumed."

"That's enough of your damned nonsense! What about this crazy guy showing his bare face? How do I know that he won't—"

"The foregoing interruption was the result of circumstances beyond the control of CentProg. Normal service will now be resumed."

Sid stared, aghast. A taped voice! A brush-off! He was supposed to settle for that? Well, by God, he had a contract...

MEL's code flashed again. Sid tuned him in. "Mel, this is a damned outrage. I called police channel and do you know what I got? A canned announcement—"

"Sid," Mel cut in. "Do you suppose it meant anything? I mean the uh...guy with the...uh face. All that about getting out, and the glacier wiping out the city."

"What?" Sid stared at Mel's pattern, trying to make sense of what he was saying. "Glacier?" he said. "Wipe out what?"

"You saw him, didn't you? The crazy bird, cut in on all channels. He said the ice was going to wipe out the city..."

Sid thought back. The damned obscene face. He hadn't really listened to what it was raving about. But it was something about getting out...

"Tell me that again, Mel."

Mel repeated the bare-faced man's warning. "Do you suppose there's anything in it? I mean, the shocks, and everything. And you can't get police channel. And I tried to tune in to Pubinf just now and I got a canned voice, just like you did..."

"It's crazy, Mel. It can't..."

"I don't know. I've tried to reach a couple of the fellows; I can't get through..."

"Mel," Sid asked suddenly. "How long has it been? I mean, how long since CentProg has been handling things?"

"What? My God, Sid, what a question. I don't know."

"A long time, eh, Mel? A lot could have happened outside."

"My contract—"

"But how do we know? I was talking to Cluster just now; we couldn't remember. I mean, how can you gauge a thing like that? We have our routine, and everything goes along, and nobody thinks about anything like...outside. Then all of a sudden—"

"I'm trying Pubinf again," Mel said. "I don't like this—"

MEL was gone. Sid tried to think. Pubinf was handing out canned brush-offs, just like Police Channel. CentProg... maybe it was okay now...

CentProg was still dark. Sid was staring at the blank screens when a new shock sent heavy vibrations through his cocoon. Sid gasped, tried to keep cool. It would pass; it wasn't anything, it couldn't be...

The vibrations built, heavy, hard shocks that drove the air from Sid's lungs, yanked painfully at arms, legs, neck, and his groin...

It was a long time before the nausea passed. Sid lay, drawing breath painfully, fighting down the vertigo. The pain—it was a help, in a way. It helped to clear his head. Something was wrong, bad wrong. He had to think now, do the right thing. It wouldn't do to panic. If only there wouldn't be another earthquake...

Something wet splattered against Sid's half-open mouth. He recoiled, automatically spitting the mucky stuff, snorting—

It was Vege-pap, gushing down from the feeding tube. Sid averted his face, felt the cool semi-liquid pattering against the cocoon, spreading over it, sloshing down the sides. Something was broken...

Sid groped for the cut-off with his tongue, gagging at the viscous mess pouring over his face. Of course, it hadn't actually touched his skin, except for his lips; the cocoon protected him. But he could feel the thick weight of it, awash in the fluid that supported the plastic cocoon. He could sense it quite clearly, flowing under him, forcing him up in the chamber as the hydrostatic balance was upset. With a shock of pain, Sid felt a set of neuro contacts along his spinal cord come taut. He gritted his teeth, felt searing agony as the contacts ripped loose.

Half the world went dark and cold. Sid was only dimly aware of the pressure against his face and chest as he pressed against the cell roof. All sensation was gone from his legs now, from his left arm, his back. His left contact screen was blank, unseeing. Groaning with the effort, Sid strained to reach out with a toe, key the emergency signal—

Hopeless. Without the boosters he could never make it. His legs were dead, paralyzed. He was helpless.

HE tried to scream, choked, fought silently in the swaddling cocoon, no longer a euphorically caressing second skin but a dead, clammy weight, binding him. He twisted, feeling unused muscles cramp at the effort, touched the lever that controlled the face-plate. It had been a long time since Sid had opened the plate. He'd had a reputation as an open-air fiend once—but that had been—he didn't know how long. The lever was stiff. Sid lunged against it again. It gave. There was a sudden lessening of pressure as the burden of Vege-pap slopped out through the opening. Sid sank away from the ceiling of the tiny cubicle, felt his cocoon ground on the bottom.

For a long time Sid lay, dazed by pain and shock, not even thinking, waiting for the agony to subside…

Then the itching began. It penetrated Sid's daze, set him twitching in a frenzy of discomfort. The tearing loose of the dorsal contacts had opened dozens of tiny rents in the cocoon; a sticky mixture of the supporting water bath and Vege-pap seeped in, irritating the tender skin. Sid writhed, struggled to scratch—and discovered that, miraculously, the left arm responded now. The motor nerves, which had been stunned by the electro-neural trickle-flow through the contacts were recovering control. Feebly, Sid's groping hand reached his inflamed hip—and scrabbled against the smooth sheath of plastic.

He had to get out. The cocoon was a confining nightmare, a dead husk that had to be shed. The face-plate was open. Sid felt upward, found the edge, tugged—

Slippery as an eel, he slithered from the cocoon, hung for an instant as the remaining contacts came taut, then slammed to the floor a foot below. Sid didn't feel the pain of the fall; as the contacts ripped free, he fainted.

WHEN Sid recovered consciousness, his first thought was that the narco channel was getting a little TOO graphic. He groped for a tuning switch—

Then he remembered. The earthquake, Mel, the canned announcement—

And he had opened his faceplate and fought to get out—and here he was. He blinked dully, then moved his left hand. It took a long time, but he managed to peel the contact screens from his eyes. He looked around. He was lying on the floor in a rectangular tunnel. A dim light came from a glowing green spot along the corridor. Sid remembered seeing it before, a long time ago...the day he and Cluster had entered their cocoons.

Now that he was detached from the stimuli of the cocoon, it seemed to Sid, he was able to think a little more clearly. It had hurt to be torn free from the security of the cocoon, but it wasn't so bad now. A sort of numbness had set in. But he couldn't lie here and rest; he had to do something, fast. First, there was Cluster. She hadn't answered. Her cocoon was situated right next to his—

Sid tried to move; his leg twitched; his arm fumbled over the floor. It was smooth and wet, gummy with the Vega-pap that was still spilling down from the open face-plate. The smell of the stuff was sickening. Irrationally, Sid had a sudden mouth-watering hunger for Prote-sim.

Sid fixed his eyes on the green light, trying to remember. He and Cluster had been wheeled along the corridor, laughing and talking gaily. Somehow, out here, things took on a different perspective. That had been—God! YEARS ago. How long? Maybe—twenty years? Longer. Fifty, maybe. Maybe longer. How could you know? For a while they had tuned to Pubinf, followed the news, kept up with friends on the outside. But more and more of their friends had signed contracts with CentProg. The news sort of dried up. You lost interest.

But what mattered now wasn't how long, it was what he was going to do. Of course, an attendant would be along soon in any case to check up, but meanwhile, Cluster might be in trouble—

THE tremor was bad this time. Sid felt the floor rock, felt the hard paving under him ripple like the surface of a pond. Somewhere, a rumbling sound rolled, and somewhere something heavy fell. The green light flickered, then burned steadily again.

A shape moved in the gloom of the corridor; there was the wet slap of footsteps. Sid sub-vocalized a calm 'Hi, fellows'— the silence rang in his ears. My God, of course they couldn't hear him. He tried again, consciously vocalizing, a tremendous shout—

A feeble croak, and a fit of coughing. When he recovered his breath, a bare and hairy face, greenish white, was bending over him.

"…this poor devil," the man was saying in a thin choked voice.

Another face appeared over the first face's shoulder. Sid recognized them both. They were the two that had been breaking into decent channels, with their wild talk about a glacier…

"Listen, fellow," one of the bare-faced men said. Sid stared with fascinated disgust at the clammy pale skin, the sprouting hairs, the loose toothless mouth, the darting pink tongue. God, people were horrible to look at!

"…be along after awhile. Didn't mean to stir up anybody in your shape. You been in too long, fellow. You can't make it."

"I'm…good…shape…" Sid whispered indignantly.

"We can't do anything for you. You'll have to wait till the maintenance unit comes along. I'm pretty sure you'll be okay. The ice's piled itself up in a wall now, and split around the city walls. I think they'll hold. Course, the ice will cover the city, but that won't matter. CentProg will still handle everything. Plenty of energy from the pile and the solar cells, and the recycling will handle the food okay…"

"…Cluster…" Sid gasped.

The bare-faced man leaned closer. Sid explained about his wife. The man checked nearby faceplates. He came back and knelt by Sid. "Rest easy, fellow," he said. "They all look all right. Your wife's okay. Now, we're going to have to go on. But you'll be okay. Plenty of Vege-pap around, I see. Just eat a little now and then. The Maintenance machine will be along and get you tucked back in."

"Where…?" Sid managed.

"Us? We're heading south. Matt here knows where we can get clothes and supplies, maybe even a flier. We never were too set on this Vital Programming. We've only been in maybe a few years and we always did a lot of auto-gym work, keeping in shape. Didn't like the idea of wasting away…Matt's the one found out about the ice. He came for me…"

Sid was aware of the other man talking. It was hard to hear him.

A sudden thought struck Sid. "…how…long…?" he asked.

IT took three tries, but the bare-faced man got the idea at last. "I'll take a look, fellow," he said. He went to Sid's open faceplate, peered at it, called the other man over. Then he came back, his feet spattering in the puddled Vege-pap.

"Your record says…2043," he said. He looked at Sid with wide eyes. They were red and irritated, Sid saw. It made his own eyes itch.

"If that's right, you been here since the beginning. My God, that's over…two hundred years…"

The second bare-faced man, Matt, was pulling the other away. He was saying something, but Sid wasn't listening. Two hundred years. It seemed impossible. But after all, why not? In a controlled environment, with no wear and tear, no disease, you could live as long as CentProg kept everything running. But two hundred years…

Sid looked around. The two men were gone. He tried to remember just what had happened, but it was too hard. The ice, they had said, wouldn't crush the city. But it would flow around it, encase it in ice, and the snow would fall, and cover it, and the City would lie under the ice.

Ages might pass. In the cells, the cocoons would keep everyone snug and happy. There would be the traditional sitcoms, and Narco, and Psychan…

And up above, the ice.

Sid remembered the awful moments in the cocoon, when the shock waves had rocked him; the black wave of fear that had closed in; the paralyzing claustrophobia.

The ice would build up and build up. Ice, two miles thick…

Why hadn't they waited? Sid groped, pushed himself up, rolled over. He was stronger already. Why hadn't they waited? He'd used the micro-spasm unit regularly—every so often. He had good muscle tone. It was just that he was a little stiff. He scrabbled at the floor, moved his body a few inches. Nothing to it. He remembered the reason for the green light; it was the elevator. They had brought him and Cluster down in it. All he had to do was get to it, and—

WHAT about Cluster? He could try to bring her along. It would be lonely to be without her. But she wouldn't want to leave. She'd been here—two hundred years. Sid almost chuckled. Cluster wouldn't like the idea of being as old as that…

No, he'd go alone. He couldn't stay, of course. It would never be the same again for him. He pulled himself along, an inch, another. He rested, sucked up some Vege-pap from where it spread near his mouth…

He went on. It was a long way to the green light, but if you took it an inch at a time, an inch at a time…

He reached the door. There hadn't been any more shocks. Along the corridor, the glass face-plates stood closed, peaceful, orderly. The mess on the floor was the only thing. But the maintenance units would be along. The bare-faced man had said so.

You opened the door to the elevator by breaking a beam of light; Sid remembered that. He raised his arm; it was getting strong, all right. It was hardly any effort to lift it right up—

The door opened with a whoosh of air. Sid worked his way inside. Halfway in, the door tried to close on him; his weight must have triggered the door-closing mechanism. But it touched him and flew open again. It was working fine, Sid thought.

He pulled his legs in, then rested. He would have to get up to the switch, somehow, and that was going to be tricky. Still, he had gotten this far okay. Just a little farther, and he'd catch up with the bare-faced men, and they'd set out together.

It took Sid an hour of hard work, but he managed to reach, first, the low stool, then the chrome-plated control button. With a lurch the car started up. Sid fell back to the floor and fought back wave on wave of vertigo. It was hectic, being outside. But he wouldn't go back now; not even to see Cluster's familiar identity pattern again. Never again. He had to get out.

The elevator came to a stop. The door slid open—and a blast of sub-arctic air struck Sid like a blow from a giant hammer. His naked body—mere flaccid skin over atrophied bones—curled like a grub in the flames. For a long moment all sensation was washed away in the shock of the cold. Then there was pain; pain that went on and on...

AND then the pain went, and it was almost like being back again, back in the cocoon, warm and comfortable, secure and protected and safe. But not quite the same. A thought stirred in Sid's mind. He pushed at the fog of cotton-wool, fought to grasp the thought that bobbed on the surface of the blissful warmth.

He opened his eyes.   Out across the white expanse of rooftops, beyond the last rim of the snow, the glittering jagged shape of the ice-face reared up, crystal blue, gigantic; and in the high arched blue-black sky, a star burned with a brilliant fire.

This was what he wanted to tell Cluster, Sid thought. This, about the deep sky, and the star, so far away—and yet a man could see it.

But it was too late now to tell Cluster, too late to tell anyone. The bare-faced men were gone. Sid was alone; alone now under the sky.

LONG ago, Sid thought, on the shore of some warm and muddy sea, some yearning sea-thing had crawled out to blink at the open sky, gulp a few breaths of burning oxygen, and die.

But not in vain. The urge to climb out was the thing. That was the force that was bigger than all the laws of nature, greater than all the distant suns blazing in their meaningless lonely splendor.

The other ones, the ones below, the secure and comfortable ones in their snug cocoons under the snow, they had lost the great urge. The thing that made a man.

But he, Sid Throndyke—he had made it.

Sid lay with his eyes on the star and the silent snow drifted over him to form a still small mound; and then the mound was buried, and then the city.

And only the ice and the star remained.

THE END

The Man from the Future

By DON WILCOX

Would a man from the future like living in our world? The answer is, he wouldn't! But here he was, from 10,950 A.D.!

DON'T get me wrong. This guy didn't lift the streetcar by himself. A dozen other fellows were heaving, and the truck that had bumped the thing off its tracks a couple of minutes before was tugging at a taut log-chain.

But it was this big innocent tan-cheeked fellow in the soft gray topcoat and hat that really muscled the car back on its tracks. Then he backed into the crowd modestly and pulled out a silk handkerchief to brush the dust off his pink hands.

Then and there opportunity knocked, and yours truly, Ham-and-Eggs Brown, jumped to answer. I sprang for the articles that spilled out of this guy's handkerchief pocket. My chance to get next to him. Something told me there was money in them biceps.

"Your notebook and money, mister—" I drew up out of the shuffle of feet to hand the fellow the silver coin and the little gray memo book—

But he was gone—practically. I saw him, half a head above the crowd, making for the sidewalk. I darted after him. The congestion caught me. I charged around two fat men and took a shortcut under a news-camera. By that time the fellow was out of sight.

I looked at the stuff in my hands. The coin went to my pocket automatically. The notebook hung disturbingly in my fingers.

I drifted into the first restaurant, turned the pages of the notebook over a plate of spaghetti. The notes were shorthand of some sort. Might as well try to read my spaghetti.

But here was a patch of neat longhand.

Must brush up on archaic writing.

The final entry was in the same legible hand:

Underwent the test. No ill effects. The time-transfer was instantaneous. Arrived at the ancient year of 1950—a 9000 year jump. Fine sunny day, but noise and smoke are terrible. Otherwise, so far so good. Must get busy at once.

I pushed my spaghetti aside, gulped my ice water, mopped my brow. The date of that entry was May 10, 10,950!

Reaching into my pocket for aspirins I found the coin. It was screwy too. Dated 10,945. And worn. The letters said, *Twenty-five Cents. America.*

Not U. S. A. Just America. I looked around to see if some gagster was watching over my shoulder. Hell, if this thing was on the level the guy that heaved that streetcar was no mere Hercules, he was a gold mine... He needed a promoter. Ham-and-Eggs Brown to the rescue. Bundle this fellow off to Hollywood—

But where would I find him? A chill hit me. Darned if I hadn't let him slide right through my lunch-hooks and lose himself among four million—

A shadow crossed my unfinished spaghetti and I looked up to see the well filled gray topcoat and hat crossing in front of me. I almost leaped.

"Steady, Ham," I said to myself. "He might be delicate. Don't scare him off. Don't—ah!"

The fellow had forgotten his check. I picked it up, started after him, at the same time glancing in his notebook for his name.

"Mr. Destinoval."

The fellow whirled and a passing waiter jumped to avoid a spill.

"Your check, Mr. Destinoval." I gave him my suavest smile. "Also the things you spilled by the streetcar."

As his hand closed over the articles I got a good look at his face. Aside from being contorted with bewilderment it was a good face, one to compare with your favorite movie hero. A trifle less heavy on the jaw, a bit bulgier on forehead. Something sensitive in his features like a well-bred racehorse. At the sound of his name his ears pinkened, his crisp eyelashes flickered.

Then he managed a smile and uttered some words too fast for me to understand, which I took to mean thank you.

"My name is Ham Brown, Mr. Destinoval—"

The introduction was lost. He was off. He strode past the cashier, never stopping to pay.

The cashier shouted and a little dried apple of a manager and two husky waiters caught their cue and bounded outdoors after him. I slapped my money down and gave chase, overtaking them approximately two pie-throws down the street.

The argument was painfully one-sided. The little dried apple waved his fists and cursed the air blue. Destinoval looked scared to death—obviously up to his ears in trouble. So I plunged.

"I'll pay it."

The glares turned on me. But as quick as J. D. Destinoval saw he was supposed to fork over his check, I put some cash with it and the matter was settled. Dried apple and bodyguard trooped off grumbling contentedly.

This time I grabbed my protege by the sleeve and hung on.

"Why'd you do it, pal? Don't you know no better?"

What he answered buzzed off his tongue fast enough to put a tobacco auctioneer to shame. I didn't get a word of it.

"Come again," I said, "or ain't you hep to English?"

He gave me the same scared eye he'd wasted on the restaurant manager and tried to pull away. I bulldogged his coat sleeve all the way to the stoplight. Then I let go. Two cops and a plainclothes on the other side of the street were looking our way hungrily.

WE backed into a doorway and my protege talked on.

"Hold it," I said. "Is that the way you talk where you come from?"

He nodded eagerly. He rattled on, pointing first to me and then to the gray memo book. His eyes brightened as we came to an understanding.

"Yes, I read a little of it," I admitted. "That's where I got your name. If you're on the level about coming back from 10,950—"

He almost hugged me he was so excited. He shook both my hands at once. Out of the wild rattle of his words I caught exactly nothing. I broke in:

"Listen, partner, you need a friend and I'm it. I'm your general manager, see?" I flashed a card at him. "Promoter, that's my business. We'll draw up a contract. But first you've got to slow down that sixteen-cylinder jabber—Quiet! We can't both talk at once… What's that…Say it again…Slow…*Slower!*"

Gradually I throttled him down and his smooth rich voice made sense.

"I'm at sea, my dear atom-smasher." He was addressing me with a term of endearment, as I later learned. "Why can't we both talk at once?"

"It's bad manners."

"Why?"

"Because when one guy's talking the other oughta listen."

"That's absurd," he said. "Can't you talk and listen at the same time?"

"Maybe *you* can," I said skeptically.

"Of course. It's perfectly good etiquette as long as not more than six talk at once. It takes five or six to round out a conversation, in my times, and nobody misses a word."

"You're back in the twentieth century now, brother," I advised. "A word to the wise. And another thing—this business of walking out on your bills—"

Anxiety flickered through his face. This was a matter he'd tried to ask about, he said, but no one had understood him. I questioned him and saw there was a trouble cloud gathering.

You see, he carried a head full of dangerous notions. They might be good for 10,950 but they were screwball for 1950.

"I supposed food was free," he said. "In my times—"

"These ain't your times," I snapped.

He squinted an eye at me.

"Do you pay to walk on the sidewalks? To sit in the parks?"

"Of course not. That's public. Everybody uses the streets and parks—"

"My point exactly," he said. "In my times everybody uses food and beds. The public pays the bill from our taxes. If a man needs a room at a hotel—"

"Great guns! Don't tell me you've walked out on a hotel bill?"

My answer came in action stronger than words. The cops and the plainclothes man had crossed the street toward us. The plainclothes, who happened to be the house dick at the Ingerbond

Hotel, thrust a thumb at my friend and muttered, "That's him. Professional deadbeat, most likely."

"We'll let the judge look into it," said a cop.

As they led him to a wagon he looked back with a hint of scare in his movie-star face and called,

"Don't forget, you're my manager."

I grabbed a car for the police station. Then remembering I was short on ready cash I backtracked, through a time-costly traffic jam, to the Daily Beacon. I brushed past the city editor and hove up at the desk labeled: VELMA MACK, SOCIETY.

"She's not in," growled Split-Infinitive, the rewrite man.

"Give her my love," I said. "Tell her bluebirds are singing. She'll get that vacation to Atlantic City. I'm taking her myself."

Split looked me up and down. "When'd your rich uncle die?"

"None of that. I've just made the discovery of the year—a man with uncanny talents—hell, he's colossal! I'm giving him six months on vaudeville—I've got an in, you know—then Hollywood."

Split lit a cigarette.

"What's his name?"

"J. D. Dest—" I considered. This man from the future needed a name that would look well in the headlines. Ah— "John Doe Destiny."

I sat down at Velma Mack's desk to write her a note. A cigar was burning in her ashtray and the aroma caught me.

"Beau Tassel's been here."

Split nodded. "His Detroit fights were called off."

"I don't like the way he comes borrowing money from Velma."

"He didn't. Just came to say he'd take her on her Atlantic City vacation—"

"*He'd* take her?" I bounced up from the chair. "Hell, that won't do. Anyway he can't swing it—"

"He was dressed up like a million."

I writhed. If Beau was sporting a new outfit, he'd dipped into our prize money again—that three hundred-dollar radio contest award that had brought him and Velma and me together in an off-the-record corporation.

"Beau claimed he'd sighted a bonanza." Split opened the noon edition to a picture of the derailed streetcar. It showed the dozen men heaving and the center one was John Doe Destiny. The staff artist had drawn a question mark on Destiny's back. The story started off.

Who is he?

Who is the mysterious Hercules that swung the streetcar back on its tracks and disappeared in the crowd before the reporters could...

The thing caught me in the ribs.

"Is that all Beau Tassel had to go on?"

"He said he'd round up this he-man and make a heavyweight champ out of him. If you ask me, Velma went along to throw a monkey-wrench."

"Went where? They'll never find him. I'm the only one who knows—"

"Don't kid yourself. One reporter over at the police station called in twenty minutes ago to say the guy they'd dumped in cell seventeen was—"

I leaped from the desk and caught up my hat on the run. Outside the door I hailed a taxi and was off.

THE cop dozing in the tilted chair inside the rear door of the station opened one eye at me. I flashed my card at him and he let the eye fall closed. I strode back to seventeen. John Doe Destiny was there. And no one else, thank goodness. I assumed that Velma and Beau hadn't come yet. I extended my friendliest hand through the bars.

"Ah my friend—"

The man from the future ignored the hand. He blew his nose into his silk handkerchief, rolled his watery eyes like a prize bull at a livestock show suffering with nostalgia. I threw in a load of good cheer.

"I'll have you out right away, old man. I've got big plans for you—no, don't thank me now. Wait till we've cleaned up—"

"I'm sick, " John Doe Destiny moaned. "I've been back in this bygone age only twenty-four hours and I've already contracted one of your deadly diseases."

I gulped.

132

"What the hell?"

"I've got a cold."

"In twenty-four hours? Must have had it coming on when you left home."

"We don't have colds back home," he blubbered. "I think I'll go back."

"Oh, no. You couldn't. You just got here. I've got to make Atlantic—er—you've got a career to think of, my boy. Come, brace up!"

"I'll probably die. I've no resistance." He took time out for sniffles. He really had 'em.

"Take it easy. Anybody in the pink like you—" I paused and turned the subject. "What kind of athlete were you back home? How'd you come to be so strong?"

"I'm just average," he said; but after I prodded him a little he opened up on his past, nine thousand years in the future. Everybody was in fine health there, he said. You had to be, or pay a fine for your negligence. He believed that scientific diet and exercise must have improved the race considerably, judging from what he had seen of us poor denizens of 1950.

While he talked I jotted a contract on an envelope. I'd get an exclusive on this mint.

"You haven't told anyone about yourself but me, have you?" I asked.

"At first I tried to tell everyone," he said, "but nobody understood. I never knew I was talking too fast till you told me."*

"I'm your doctor, J. D. Put your trust in me. Your whirlwind talk and streetcar lifting and ability to hear six conversations will make you a topnotch attraction. Six months of footlights, then klieg. Sign here, Desty, and we'll transpose it onto sheepskin later."

He reached through the bars but didn't take the pen. He patted me on the shoulder.

"Brown, you're a real atom-buster. Tonight when I flash back through time I'll remember you as my best friend from these ancient days."

I WAS touched. The fellow was both sick and homesick. The bitter truth was, he'd got his stomach full of the twentieth century in twenty-four hours.

Besides his cold, he'd filled up on smoke and dust. He'd listened to more terrifying traffic noises, witnessed more near-accidents, seen more people that looked like escapees from madhouses, heard more stupid slow-motion conversation, seen more evidence of outlandish superstitions, than he had ever supposed a civilization could be guilty of possessing.

Beyond that, he'd crashed into some silly laws and got himself jailed. The humiliation of it! All before he'd had time to get his bearings.

"All because you didn't meet the right people," I said. "I'll make your troubles melt like snowflakes."

"Snowflakes!" he groaned. "It's all a blinding blizzard. If I survive this cold there are a thousand other diseases. The sanitation's abominable!" He paced his cell, a shaken man. "Already I've been hounded by a mouse in this very room. And this morning in my hotel I was awakened to find a deadly little winged beast hovering over me, the kind I've read about in horror stories of the past—a housefly."

He closed his eyes at the hideous thought. I tried to comfort him but he was off on another depressing rhapsody.

"How can I endure all this money madness? It's money, money, every time I turn around."

I tackled him on that point. How could he expect to come back and share this century's blessings (he raised a dubious eyebrow at my term) unless he contributed something?

----

*It has actually been proven that it is possible to increase the speed of speech until it is almost impossible to follow the words. And yet, when it is recorded, and played back slowly, it does not reveal a slurring or omission of words. Some types of nervous disorders result in this quickening of the speech. The man from the future is probably taught from birth to speak with great rapidity, and thus, his hearing is also trained to distinguish between the syllables. But, if you have this ability today, it might be a good idea to go on the vaudeville stage!—Ed.

That nettled him. He had come with a purpose. He hinted at some far-flung research that I wouldn't understand.

"Perfectly clear," I said. "Sign here and I'll see that you earn all you need. You can even start an anti-mouse campaign—"

A voice back of me broke in.

"Don't sign anything, Buddy. I've got you all fixed up."

I turned to glare into the massaged face of Beau Tassel. He strode up in a sprucy blue suit and blue hat with a yellow feather, and tapped a new white cane against the bars.

"I've phoned some pals to get a fight booked. I'll have you out of that cold and in training togs before you know it, Buddy."

Back of Beau came the snappy heel-click of Velma Mack. Maybe it was the extra rouge on her pretty face but she looked a little mad. At Beau, I hoped.

"You can't do it, Beau! He's too refined. He's a natural for culture lectures to high society. And for heaven's sakes quit calling him Buddy... 'Lo, Ham." She added the greeting as if I were an inconsequential part of the scenery.

John Doe Destiny gave a nasal bark that should have settled the matter.

"I don't wish to fight, Mr. Tassel."

"There!" Velma gloated. "I'll take him in hand. I'll see that he meets the best people."

"What goes on?" I roared. "He's mine—my own John Doe Destiny—booked for vaudeville—then Hollywood—"

"Since when?" Beau demanded, suddenly noticing me.

"I'm his manager. I found him. I discovered he has talents—more of 'em than the law allows in a prizefighter."

THAT blew Beau's lid off. The three of us cut loose in a three-way verbal fight. John Doe Destiny perked up. All of us talking at top speed made him feel more at home. He didn't miss a word. Me, all I got was that Beau and Velma had been here ahead of me and had learned he'd come back from the future and had tried to contaminate his ambitions. I shouted for my rights.

"I was first, wasn't I, John Doe? Didn't I show you my card?"

The hog-calling effects of our argument carried down the corridor. The cop jogged to his feet and stomped toward us. I lowered my voice.

"I agreed to be your manager—"

"But your card," John Doe Destiny cut in with a broad smile, "was an awful fake, my dear atom-buster."

This jolted me. I remembered having flashed the card under his eyes an instant so that he'd see nothing but a blur. The old Ham Brown technique.

"To be precise, Brown," John Doe followed through, "your card read, 'Social Security Act, account number 323- 16-4475, Hamilton J. Brown, unemployed.' Your sleight-of-hand may do for this century, but nine thousand years of fast-moving civilization have quickened my eyesight."

You should have heard the silence. Of all the uncanny wallops this man packed, this was the startlingest. The three of us gaped, Velma and Beau being familiar with the nature of Ham Brown card flashes.

The cop broke the silence with the noise of scratching his head in an inspired manner. He opened his billfold and gave John Doe Destiny an eyewink's look. Then, "What'd you see?"

John Doe raised his brows, lowered his lids, and recited:

"Driver's License. Name of Operator, Jason McCudahey. Number 29792633. Street address…"

He read back every word of it. Right out of his mind. Darned if he hadn't photographed the thing with his eyes!

A strange light came into the cop's face. He started off, then came back and shook a finger at Destiny.

"Stay where you are, young fellow, till I see the chief. I figure the force can use you."

"I'm going back home," Destiny called after him, but the cop pounded away.

Velma, Beau, and I exchanged glances and came to our senses. No more argument. High time to settle on one plan before this bird flew out of our hands. We took ourselves back into a huddle.

"Co-operation's the word," I said. "Which'll it be—vaudeville star, socialite, or pugilist?"

"Grab for it," said Velma, taking Beau's cane and holding it up. We grabbed, hand over hand. Beau's hand topped us.

"He's a prizefighter," said Beau.

WE TALKED our protege past the judge before the police chief came around with any tempting offers, so John Doe Destiny was all ours. Our pooled cash took care of all claims. We marched down the steps, arms linked through Destiny's, in the spirit of treasure hunters lugging a chest of uncounted gold.

We piled into the car Beau Tassel had rented, hesitated just long enough to toss the reporters a few salty statistics to make the public mouth water, and shoved off. Destiny heaved a big sigh.

"No workouts before tomorrow," said Beau. "A fresh-air ride's the thing for that cold."

"Anything to keep him entertained," Velma whispered to me.

I patted her hand. I knew her heart was set on that Atlantic City vacation. Well, we weren't going to let this golden bird fly back home nine thousand years out of reach. Fact was, we were becoming attached to the fellow.

"You'll like our little city," said Beau in the charming voice he'd practiced on Velma the last few weeks. "Nice little city."

Definitely the wrong tack. I tried to give Beau the high sign but he was too busy running stoplights. The stubborn mullethead, he drove through all the newspaper-strewn parks, skyscraper canyons and smoky railroad yards—a chamber of horrors to John Doe Destiny. To make it worse, Beau threw in a lecture. On that corner six gangsters were shot. In this block a tenement house burned to the ground one night and legend has it that some of the sleepers never woke up.

"Beau, for heaven's sakes, it's getting late," Velma would wail from the back seat.

"It's never late when we've got a guest like Mr. Buddy Destiny," Beau would retort with a big-hearted laugh.

John Doe Destiny became nauseated. Frequently we passed blocks of slums. Our protests bounced off Beau like punches off a champion. To cap the climax he wound up with a tour around the stockyards.

We put Destiny to be a shattered man.

I sat up all night to be sure he didn't fly off to his own century—though I couldn't have blamed him much.

BY THE end of the week John Doe Destiny was fairly well under control. A whopping fight was billed for a Friday only two weeks away. This Killer Metheny was a big name and would draw a fat gate.

And maybe you think the newspapers and radio commentators didn't do right by our Buddy Destiny? Sports writers took this future business for an A-1 publicity gag; the public took it for a hoax. But nobody cared to stick his neck out. The evidence was too solid that John Doe was straight goods.

The newspapers headlined him as Buddy Destiny, the two-fisted forebodie of the year ten-thousand, the man with the watermelon biceps, the handsomest guy that would ever leap into a ring. (He'd never been in one before.)

Dopesters gave Killer the edge because they'd seen him fight. They said experience would tell.

We were sure of Buddy on the same grounds. Nine thousand years of experience weren't to be sneezed at.

Yep, Buddy Destiny had an advantage that the Killer camp completely ignored: ninety centuries of upbuilding of the human race into something sturdier, quicker, more sensitive—

There was the loophole!

John Doe Destiny didn't want to fight. He abhorred it. He'd never seen a prizefight and he hoped to keep that record clean. Where he came from people were genteel and delicate.

He took to roadwork and punching bags like a veteran. He outclassed Beau in rope skipping after the first hour. It was marvelous the way his habits clicked into place, once he was shown. The same as he'd learned to slow down his speech.

But could you get that guy into a ring with a sparring partner? No.

"I wouldn't care to hit any man," he would say. "Even if I were angry, I'd settle it some other way."

Every night after we got the fellow to sleep, Beau and I would have coffee with Velma and try to figure the thing out.

"The winner'll make off with seventy percent," Beau moaned.

"If we lose, Atlantic City is off my calendar, that's all," said Velma resignedly, looking at us like a beautiful lady on a poster appealing for funds. "Your fair-haired boy knows how to count money. He's made out a budget. Out of thirty percent we'll get expenses only—if he fights."

"But if he wins, Velma," I said, "I'm taking you to Atlantic City."

"I'm ahead of you, son," said Beau suavely.

"If he wins, you'll both take me." Velma divided a peach marmalade smile between us. But Beau pulled the gloom cloud over us again.

"How'll we ever get him to fight? Every time I argue the matter he threatens me. Says he'll hop for home."

Velma lowered her eyelids as if maybe she had a glimmer.

"If he's never swung at a partner," I suggested, "how do you know he packs a wallop?"

"We'll know tomorrow," said Beau. "The Detroit A. A. is bringing over their famous striking meter. If he can hit a ten he can deliver a knockout."

Beau was being optimistic. Killer Metheny had struck a thirty-two.

THE next day the truck unloaded the meter at our back door and a circle of reporters helped roll it to the center of the gym floor. I looked around for John Doe Destiny.

He was standing by the window in trunks and gloves, a sunshiny mountain of handsome muscles, having a chat with Velma. I sauntered over.

"What do you remember most from that car ride?" Velma was asking him. A look of pain shot through his face.

"I remember everything," he said. "But the most heartrending sight was that three story firetrap at 7892¼ Manodene Street, with fourteen ragged children playing on the walk in front of it, and six broken windows patched with newspapers and rags—"

"Would you like those children to have a better home?"

A quick light came into Destiny's eyes.

"Do I have anything to say about that?"

"You could offer to build them a decent house if you had the money."

Beau Tassel interrupted, calling Destiny over to the striking meter. We all crowded around.

"Don't be afraid of hitting too hard," said Beau. "The world's champ did forty-eight. That still leaves half the dial. Go ahead, Buddy."

Destiny gave the thing a wallop. The dial jumped to three. The sports writers groaned and I, for one, felt an awful emptiness in the stomach.

Tassel snapped the dial down and tried to quiet the uproar among the on lookers. Their harsh talk cut John Doe to the quick. An assistant trainer's muttered oath acted on him like a foul blow. Velma pushed into the circle and made the assistant apologize and after a few minutes we persuaded Destiny to try again.

"Hit it as hard as you can," Velma said.

Destiny lashed out. There was an awful clang and the meter crumpled back and splashed metal parts all over the floor. Nothing was left of the dial. John Doe Destiny blushed and, backed away, saying that if they didn't mind he'd like to be excused to continue a conversation with Velma about a house.

WELL, this was the big night. We kept our dressing room door closed to the last minute. The uproar was terribly jarring to Destiny's delicate nerves. He shuddered and paced the floor all through the preliminaries.

"They're hitting each other," he would chant with his eyes closed. "They're mauling each other with their fists." Then he would turn to Beau and me and plead, "Do I actually have to strike my opponent to win this fight?"

"Just once," Beau would answer.

Our call came. We jammed plugs in Destiny's ears and hoped the shouting wouldn't terrify him too much. We ushered him through the jam-packed aisle to his corner.

The announcer introduced Killer Metheny in glowing terms. Then he led John Doe Destiny to the center of the ring and sang out:

"They say he comes back from ten-nine-fifty, and what a nifty! His punch is a sensation to jolt you future generations! Ho-de-ho-de, the two-fisted forebodie, Buddy Destiny!"

Tumultuous applause and shouting. Velma Mack at my elbow chewed gum and pounded her hands like mad.

The fight was on. The gong brought Killer Metheny prancing out of his corner like a champ. He crouched, sprang, threw a volley of punches at the air. But he didn't hit anything.

Buddy Destiny eluded him, sneaking out of reach with clever footwork that had the crowd gasping. Killer couldn't close the gap. Round one ended without a blow landed.

Destiny skipped back to his corner but he didn't sit. For some strange reason he just stood there surveying the crowd. Then he bent down to Beau Tassel.

"What are the gate receipts?"

Beau said he didn't know.

"Find out," said Destiny. "I don't want to fight unless I can make all I need to build a house."

He went back into Round two, and Beau turned to Velma and me with a gray face.

"The guy's out of his head."

"Don't you believe it," said Velma. "Go find out about that gate, and hurry."

Round two was like Round one, but fast. It ended with Killer madder than a bull because he hadn't been able to connect. The crowd was heating.

Round three was a footrace spiced with the most amazing demonstration of ducking and dodging you ever saw. Buddy Destiny came back to his corner without being touched. But he looked sick. The boos were cutting him down. The crowd was all for Killer now. They wanted to see a fight.

Just before Round four Beau returned looking pale and scared. "Destiny, you've got to knock him out by the fifth. I can't tell you why but you've got to. This time get in there and—"

Velma gave Beau a restraining pinch on the arm. Destiny only said, "How much was the gate?"

Beau gave him the figure.

"It's not enough," said Destiny. "I counted the crowd at the end of Round one and checked my figures during Rounds two and three."

"A knockout by Round five!" Beau wailed.

"Go back and make them straighten up those accounts," said Destiny. "I won't strike a blow till you do."

ROUND four looked bad. Yes, there were limits to tricky footwork and dodging, not to mention hurdling, even for the versatile Destiny. He slowed down a little, used his guard more, took a glancing blow here and there. Killer was getting onto him at last, and did the crowd love it!

Still John Doe Destiny refused to strike a blow. His own camp groaned. Velma yelled at him wildly. The gong at the end of Round four was welcome music.

And the return of Beau Tassel, looking as eager as dynamite, was a welcome sight.

"You were right, Buddy. Someone tried to hold back part of the gate. The quick check-up caught him. Now, Buddy-boy, how about it?"

"Remember those poor little kids!" Velma cried into Destiny's plugged ears. "Think of that new home, all the good you can do with that extra dough—"

She was still shouting as Destiny went into Round five. She shouted for undernourished kids, for orphans, for widows, for homeless cats—

All at once you could see the imagination working in Destiny's face. His memory of the house with the patched windows set him off like a trigger. He walked into Killer Metheny.

The surprise action took the crowd for a hush.

Then—*spat.*

Killer Metheny bounced into the ropes and hung there with the most completely cockeyed expression I ever saw. Probably an all time high in cockeyed expressions, judging by the way the crowd hit the ceiling. Technically, Killer wasn't down. That is, the ropes wouldn't let him down. But he was completely out.

Under the deafening roar the baffled referee took the situation in. What a picture! Destiny's photographic memory would preserve this one for a chuckle of pride nine thousand years hence—

But I was wrong. What John Doe Destiny saw was the stream of blood that oozed harmlessly from the nose of the veteran pugilist.

"*I did it*," Destiny gasped. He fainted dead away and fell on his back in the center of the ring. The referee bent over him and counted him out.

IT WAS noon the next day when a loud knocking awakened me. I roused up and let Beau Tassel in. He looked like something wild and hunted.

"Have you seen Buddy Destiny?"

"No," I said. "What about him?"

"Gone."

"Gone where?"

I wished I hadn't asked the question, it brought such a whipped look to Beau's face. He turned away and jammed his cigar in an ashtray. I tried to smooth things over.

"Too bad. He was a good guy."

"Yeah...No fighter, though."

"No, no fighter... Didn't he even leave a note?"

"He left nothing," said Beau, "except a check to cover training expenses. That and a fund for a new house for some slum kids. That rounded out his thirty percent."

"Have you told Velma?"

Beau shook his head. I sensed that he was holding back something. I quizzed him and he admitted it. The plunger, he'd bet the last of our radio prize money that Destiny would win by the fifth. No wonder he didn't want to face Velma.

"We'd better tell her, the sooner the better," I said, so we made tracks for the Daily Beacon.

"Is she in?" Beau asked.

"Does her desk look it?" retorted Split-Infinitive. It didn't. It was heaped high with mail. "Fan letters," said Split, "on that special society broadcast she put over with your John Doe Destiny night before last."

Broadcast? We hadn't heard of any broadcast. Beau turned a little purple.

"She said Destiny needed some intellectual diversion or he'd go back home," said Split. "She had him do a lecture on the future of culture and refinement."

I fought for a deep breath.

"Do they get paid for that stuff?"

Split smiled. "And how. Velma's got an advance for a whole series. You men should listen in. There'll be talks on the decay of vaudeville and the death of pugilism—"

Beau gave a deep growl.

"Tell me, how can he give any more lectures? He's gone."

"He'll be back from Atlantic City in a couple weeks," said Split. "He told me to tell you."

THE END

Letter of the Law

By ALAN E. NOURSE

Survival of the fittest, on the frontier planet of Altair, was a matter of who could tell the biggest whopper. Con man Harry Zeckler considered himself a real master of the art—but he didn't know the Altairians!

THE PLACE was dark and damp, and smelled like moldy leaves. Meyerhoff followed the huge, bearlike Altairian guard down the slippery flagstones of the corridor, sniffing the dead, musty air with distaste. He drew his carefully tailored, Terran-styled jacket closer about his shoulders, shivering as his eyes avoided the black, yawning cell-holes they were passing. His foot had slipped on the slimy flags from time to time, and finally he paused to wipe the caked mud from his trouser leg. "How much farther is it?" he shouted angrily.

The guard waved a heavy paw vaguely into the blackness ahead. Quite suddenly the corridor took a sharp bend, and the Altairian stopped, producing a huge key ring from some obscure fold of his hairy hide. "I still don't see any reason for all the fuss," he grumbled in a wounded tone. "We've treated him like a brother—"

One of the huge steel doors clicked open. Meyerhoff peered into the blackness, catching a vaguely human outline against the back wall. "Harry?" he called sharply.

There was a startled gasp from within, and a skinny, gnarled little man suddenly appeared in the guard's light, like a grotesque, twisted ghost out of the blackness. Wide blue eyes regarded Meyerhoff from beneath uneven black eyebrows, and then the little man's face broke into a crafty grin. "Paul! So they sent *you!* I knew I could count on it!" He executed a deep, awkward bow, motioning Meyerhoff into the dark cubicle.

"Not much to offer you," he said slyly, "but it's the best I can do under the circumstances…"

Meyerhoff scowled, and turned abruptly to the guard. "We'll have some privacy now, if you please. Interplanetary ruling. And leave us the light."

The guard grumbled, and started for the door. "It's about time you showed up!" cried the little man in the cell. "Great day! Lucky they sent you, pal. Why, I've been in here for years—"

"Look, Zeckler—the name is Meyerhoff, and I'm not your pal," Meyerhoff snapped. "And you've been here for two weeks, three days, and approximately four hours. You're getting as bad as your gentle guards when it comes to bandying the truth around." He peered through the dim light at the gaunt face of the prisoner. Zeckler's face was dark with a week's beard, and his bloodshot eyes belied the cocky grin on his lips. His clothes were smeared and sodden, streaked with great splotches of mud and moss. Meyerhoff's face softened a little. "So Harry Zeckler's in a jam again," he said. "You *look* as if they'd treated you like a brother."

The little man snorted. "These overgrown teddy-bears don't know what brotherhood means, nor humanity, either. Bread and water I've been getting, nothing more, and then only if they feel like bringing it down." He sank wearily down on the rock bench along the wall. "I thought you'd never get here. I sent an appeal to the Terran Consulate the first day I was arrested. What happened? I mean, all they had to do was get a man over here, get the extradition papers signed, and provide transportation off the planet for me. Why so much time? I've been sitting here rotting—" He broke off in mid-sentence and stared at Meyerhoff. "You *brought* the papers, didn't you? I mean, we can leave now?"

Meyerhoff stared at the little man with a mixture of pity and disgust. "You are a prize fool," he said finally. "Did you know that?"

Zeckler's eyes widened. "What do you mean, fool? So I spend a couple of weeks in this pneumonia-trap? The deal was worth it! I've got three million credits sitting in the Terran Consulate on Altair IV, just waiting for me to walk in and pick it up. Three million credits—do you hear? That's enough to set me up for life!"

Meyerhoff nodded grimly. "*If* you live long enough to walk in and pick it up, that is."

"What do you mean, *if?*"

MEYERHOFF sank down beside the man, his voice a tense whisper in the musty cell. "I mean that right now you are practically dead. You may not know it, but you are. You walk into a newly opened planet with your smart little bag of tricks, with a shaky passport and no permit, with no knowledge of the natives outside of two paragraphs of inaccuracies in the Explorer's Guide—and then you're not content to come in here and sell something legitimate, something the natives might conceivably be able to use. No, nothing so simple for you. You have to pull your usual high-pressure stuff. And this time, buddy, you're paying the piper."

"You mean I'm not being extradited?"

Meyerhoff grinned unpleasantly. "I mean precisely that. You've committed a crime here—a major crime. The Altairians are sore about it. And the Terran Consulate isn't willing to sell all the trading possibilities here down the river just to get you out of a mess. You're going to stand trial—and these natives are out to get you. Personally, I think they're going to get you."

Zeckler stood up shakily. "You can't believe anything the natives say," he said uneasily. "They're pathological liars. Why, you should see what they tried to sell *me!* You've never seen such a pack of liars as these critters." He glanced up at Meyerhoff. "They'll probably drop a little fine on me and let me go."

"A little fine of one Terran neck." Meyerhoff grinned nastily. "You've committed the most heinous crime these creatures can imagine, and they're going to get you for it if it's the last thing they do. I'm afraid, my friend, that your con man days are over."

Zeckler fished in the other man's pocket, extracted a cigarette, and lighted it with trembling fingers. "It's bad, then," he said finally.

"It's bad, all right."

Some shadow of the sly, elfin grin crept over the little con man's face. "Well, at any rate, I'm glad they sent you over," he said weakly. "Nothing like a good lawyer to handle a trial—"

"*Lawyer?* Not me! Oh, no—sorry, but no thanks." Meyerhoff's face beamed maliciously. "I'm your *advisor,* old boy. Nothing else. I'm here to keep you from botching things up still worse for the Trading Commission that's all. I wouldn't get tangled up in a mess with these creatures for anything!" He shook his head. "You're your own lawyer, Mr. Super-Salesman. It's all your show. And you'd better get your head out of the sand, or you're going to lose a case like it's never been lost before!"

MEYERHOFF watched the little man's pale face, and grinned inwardly. In a way, he thought, it was a pity to see such a change in the rosy-cheeked, dapper, cocksure little man who had talked his way glibly in and out of more jams than Meyerhoff could count. Trading brought scalpers; it was almost inevitable that where rich and unexploited trading ground was uncovered, it would first fall prey to the fast-trading boys. They spread out from Terra with the first wave of exploration—the slick, fast-talking men who could work new territories unfettered by the legal restrictions that soon closed down the more established planets. The first men in were the richest out, and through some curious quirk of the Terrestrial mind, they knew they could always count on Terran protection, however crooked and underhanded their methods.

But occasionally a situation arose where the civilization and social practices of the lien victims made it unwise to tamper.

Altair had been recognized at once by the Trading Commission as a commercial prize of tremendous value, but early reports had warned of the danger of wildcat trading on the little, musty, jungle-like planet with its shaggy, three-eyed inhabitants— warned specifically against the confidence tactics so frequently used—but there was always somebody, Meyerhoff reflected sourly, who just didn't get the word.

Zeckler puffed nervously on his cigarette, his narrow face a study in troubled concentration. "But I didn't *do* anything!" he exploded finally. "So I pulled an old con game. So what! Why should they get so excited? So I clipped a few thousand fast credits, pulled a little fast business." He shrugged eloquently, spreading his hands. "Everybody's doing it. They do it to each other without batting an eye. You should *see* these critters operate on each other. Why, my little scheme was peanuts by comparison—"

Meyerhoff pulled a pipe from his pocket, and began stuffing the bowl with infinite patience. "And precisely *what sort* of con game was it?" he asked quietly.

Zeckler shrugged again. "The simplest, tiredness, moldiest old racket that ever made a quick nickel. Remember the old Terran gag about the Brooklyn Bridge? The same thing. Only these critters didn't want bridges. They wanted land—this gooey, slimy swamp they call 'farmland.' So I gave them what they wanted. I just sold them some land."

Meyerhoff nodded fiercely. "You sure did. A hundred square kilos at a swipe. Only you sold the same hundred square kilos to a dozen different natives!" Suddenly he threw back his hands and roared. "Of all the things you *shouldn't* have done—"

"But what's a chunk of land?"

Meyerhoff shook his head hopelessly. "If you hadn't been so greedy, you'd have found out what a chunk of land was to these natives before you started peddling it. You'd have found out other things about them, too. You'd have learned that in spite of all their bumbling and fussing and squabbling they're not so dull. You'd have found out that they're marsupials and that two

149

out of five of them get thrown out of their mother's pouch before they're old enough to survive. You'd have realized that they have to start fighting for individual rights almost as soon as they're born. Anything goes, as long as it benefits them as individuals."

Meyerhoff grinned at the little man's horrified face. "Never heard of that, had you? And you've never heard of other things, too. You've probably never heard that there are just too many Altairians here for the food their planet can supply, and their diet is so finicky that they just can't live on anything that doesn't grow here. And consequently, land is the key factor in their economy. Not money, nothing but land.

"To get land, it's every man for himself, and the loser starves, and their entire legal and monetary system revolves on that principal. And they've built up the most confusing and impossible system of barter and trade imaginable, aimed at individual survival, with land as the value behind the credit. That explains the lying—of course they're liars, with an economy like that. They've completely missed the concept of truth.

"Pathological? You *bet* they're pathological. Only a fool would tell the truth when his life depended on his being a better liar than the next guy! Lying is the time-honored tradition, with their entire legal system built around it—"

ZECKLER snorted. "But how could they *possibly* have a legal system? I mean, if they don't recognize the truth when it slaps them in the face?"

Meyerhoff shrugged. "As we understand legal systems, I suppose they don't have one. They have only the haziest idea what truth represents, and they've shrugged off the idea as impossible and useless." He chuckled maliciously. "So you went out and found a chunk of ground in the uplands, and sold it to a dozen separate, self-centered, half-starved natives! Encroachment on private property is legal grounds for murder on this planet, and twelve of them descended on the same

150

chunk of land at the same time, all armed with title-deeds—" Meyerhoff sighed. "You've got twelve mad Altairians in your hair. You've got a mad planet in your hair. And in the meantime, Terra's most valuable uranium strike in five centuries is threatening to cut off supply unless they see your blood splattered liberally all the way from here to the equator."

Zeckler was visibly shaken. "Look," he said weakly. "So I wasn't so smart—what am I going to do? I mean, are you going to sit quietly by and let them butcher me? How could I defend myself in a legal setup like this?"

Meyerhoff smiled coolly. "You're going to get your sly little con man brain to working, I think," he said softly. "By Interplanetary Rules, they have to give you a trial in Terran legal form—judge, jury, court procedure, all that folderol. They think it's a big joke—after all, what could a judicial oath mean to them?—but they agreed. Only thing is, they're going to hang you, if they die trying. So you'd better get those stunted little wits of yours to clicking—and if you try to implicate me, even a little bit, I'll be out of there so fast you won't know what happened."

With that, Meyerhoff chuckled and strolled to the door. He jerked it inward sharply, and spilled three guards over on their faces. "Privacy," he grunted, and started back up the slippery corridor.

IT CERTAINLY looked like a courtroom, at any rate. In the front of the long, damp stone room was a bench, with a seat behind it, and a small straight chair to the right. To the left was a stand with twelve chairs—larger chairs, with a railing running along the front. The rest of the room was filled almost to the door with seats facing the bench. Zeckler followed the shaggy-haired guard into the room, nodding approvingly. "Not such a bad arrangement," he said. "They must have gotten the idea fast."

Meyerhoff wiped the perspiration from his forehead and shot the little con man a stony glance. "At least you've got a

courtroom, a judge, and a jury for this mess. Beyond that—"
He shrugged eloquently. "I can't make any promises."

In the back of the room a door burst open with a bang.
Loud, harsh voices were heard as half a dozen huge Altairians
attempted to push through the door at once. Zeckler clamped
on the headset to his translator unit, and watched the hubbub in
the anteroom with growing alarm. Finally the question of
precedence seemed to be settled, and a group of the Altairians
filed into the room in order of stature, stalking across the room
in flowing black robes, pug-nosed faces glowering in self-
importance. They descended upon the jury box, grunting and
scrapping with each other for the first-row seats, and the judge
took his place with obvious satisfaction behind the heavy
wooden bench. Finally the prosecuting attorney appeared,
flanked by two clerks, who took their places beside him. The
prosecutor eyed Zeckler with cold malevolence, then turned and
delivered a sly wink at the judge.

In a moment the room was a hubbub as it filled with the
huge, bumbling, bearlike creatures, jostling each other and
fighting for seats, growling and complaining. Two small fights
broke out in the rear, but were quickly subdued by the group of
gendarmes guarding the entrance. Finally the judge glared down
at Zeckler with all three eyes and pounded the bench top with a
wooden mallet until the roar of activity subsided. The jurymen
wriggled uncomfortably in their seats, exchanging winks, and
finally turned their attention to the front of the court.

"We are reading the case of the people of Altair I," the
judge's voice roared out, "against one Harry Zeckler—" he
paused for a long, impressive moment—"Terran." The
courtroom immediately burst into an angry growl, until the
judge pounded the bench five or six times more. "This—
creature—is hereby accused of the following crimes," the judge
bellowed. "Conspiracy to overthrow the government of Altair I.
Brutal murder of seventeen law-abiding citizens of the village of
Karzan at the third hour before dawn in the second period after
his arrival. Desecration of the Temple of our beloved Goddess

Zermat, Queen of the Harvest. Conspiring with the lesser gods to cause the unprecedented drought in the Dermatti section of our fair globe. Obscene exposure of his pouch-marks in a public square. Four separate and distinct charges of jailbreak and bribery—" the judge pounded the bench for order— "Espionage with the accursed scum of Altair II in preparation for interplanetary invasion—"

The little con man's jaw sagged lower and lower, the color draining from his face. He turned, wide-eyed, to Meyerhoff, then back to the judge.

"The chairman of the jury," said the judge succinctly, "will read the verdict."

The little native in the front of the jury box popped up like a puppet on a string. "Defendant found guilty on all counts," he said.

"Defendant is guilty! The court will pronounce sentence—"

"Now wait a minute!" Zeckler was on his feet, wild-eyed. "What kind of railroad job—"

The judge blinked disappointedly at Paul Meyerhoff. "Not yet?" he asked, unhappily.

"No." Meyerhoff's hands twitched nervously. "Not yet, your honor. Later, your honor. The trial comes *first.*"

THE JUDGE looked as if his candy had been stolen. "But you *said* I should call for the verdict—"

"Later. You have to have the trial before you can have the verdict."

The Altairian shrugged indifferently. "Now...later..." he muttered.

"Have the prosecutor call his first witness," said Meyerhoff.

Zeckler leaned over, his face ashen. "These charges," he hissed. *"They're insane!"*

"Of course they are," Meyerhoff hissed back.

"But what am I going to—"

"Sit tight. Let *them* set things up."

"But those lies. They're liars, the whole pack of them—" He broke off as the prosecutor roared a name.

The shaggy brute who took the stand was wearing a bright purple hat, which sat rakishly over one ear. He grinned the Altairian equivalent of a hungry grin at the prosecutor. Then he cleared his throat and started: "This Terran riffraff—"

"The oath," muttered the judge. "We've got to have the oath."

The prosecutor nodded, and four natives moved forward, carrying huge inscribed marble slabs to the front of the court. One by one the chunks were reverently piled in a heap at the witness's feet. The witness placed a huge, hairy paw on the cairn, and the prosecutor said, "Do you swear to tell the truth, the whole truth, and nothing but the truth, so help you—" He paused to squint at the paper in his hand, and finished on a puzzled note, "—Goddess?"

The witness removed the paw from the rock pile long enough to scratch his ear. Then he replaced it, and replied, "Of course," in an injured tone.

"Then tell this court what you have seen of the activities of this abominable wretch."

The witness settled back into the chair, fixing one eye on Zeckler's face, another on the prosecutor, and closing the third as if in meditation. "I think it was on the fourth night of the seventh crossing of Altair II (may the Goddess cast a drought upon it)—or was it the seventh night of the fourth crossing?—" he grinned apologetically at the judge—"when I was making my way back through town toward my blessed land-plot, minding my own business, your honor, after weeks of bargaining for the crop I was harvesting. Then suddenly from the shadow of a building, this creature—" he waved his paw at Zeckler— "stopped me in my tracks with a vicious cry. He had a weapon I'd never seen before, and before I could find my voice he forced me back against the wall. I could see by the crud glint in his eyes that there was no warmth, no sympathy in his heart, that I was—"

"Objection!" Zeckler squealed plaintively, jumping to his feet. "This witness can't even remember what night he's talking about!"

The judge looked startled. Then he pawed feverishly through his bundle of notes. "Overruled," he said abruptly. "Continue, please."

The witness glowered at Zeckler. "As I was saying before this loutish interruption," he muttered, "I could see that I was face to face with the most desperate of criminal types, even for Terrans. Note the shape of his head, the flabbiness of his ears! I was petrified with fear. And then, helpless as I was, this two-legged abomination began to shower me with threats of evil to my blessed home, dark threats of poisoning my land unless I would tell him where he could find the resting place of our blessed Goddess—"

"I never saw him before in my life," Zeckler moaned to Meyerhoff. "Listen to him. Why should I care where their Goddess—"

Meyerhoff gave him a stony look. "The Goddess runs things around here. She makes it rain. If it doesn't rain, somebody's insulted her. It's very simple."

"But how can I fight testimony like that?"

"I doubt if you *can* fight it."

"But they can't prove a word of it..." He looked at the jury, who were listening enraptured to the second witness on the stand. This one was testifying regarding the butcherous slaughter of eighteen (or was it twenty-three? Oh, yes, twenty-three) women and children in the suburban village of Karzan. The pogrom, it seemed, had been accomplished by an energy weapon, which ate great, gaping holes in the sides of buildings. A third witness took the stand, continuing the drone as the room grew hotter and muggier. Zeckler grew paler and paler, his eyes turning glassy as the testimony piled up. "But it's not *true,*" he whispered to Meyerhoff.

"Of course it isn't! Can't you understand? *These people have no regard for truth.* It's stupid, to them, silly, a mark of low intelligence. The only thing in the world they have any respect for is a liar bigger and more skillful than they are—"

ZECKLER jerked around abruptly as he heard his name bellowed out. "Does the defendant have anything to say before the jury delivers the verdict?"

"Do I have—" Zeckler was across the room in a flash, his pale cheeks suddenly taking on a feverish glow. He sat down gingerly on the witness chair, facing the judge, his eyes bright with fear and excitement. "Your—your honor, I—I have a statement to make, which will have a most important bearing on this case. You must listen with the greatest care." He glanced quickly at Meyerhoff, and back to the judge. "Your honor," he said in a hushed voice, "you are in gravest of danger. All of you. Your lives—your very land is at stake."

The judge blinked, and shuffled through his notes hurriedly as a murmur arose in the court. "Our land?"

"Your lives, your land, everything you hold dear," Zeckler said quickly, licking his lips nervously. "You must try to understand me—" he glanced apprehensively over his shoulder—"now, because I may not live long enough to repeat what I am about to tell you—"

The murmur quieted down, all ears straining in their headsets to hear his words. "These charges," he continued, "all of them—they're perfectly true. At least, they seem to be perfectly true. But in every instance, I was working with heart and soul, risking my life, for the welfare of your beautiful planet."

There was a loud hiss from the back of the court. Zeckler frowned and rubbed his hands together. "It was my misfortune," he said, "to go to the wrong planet when I first came to Altair from my homeland on Terra. I—I landed on Altair II, a grave mistake, but as it turned out, a very fortunate error. Because in attempting to arrange trading in that frightful place, I made certain contacts." His voice trembled, and sank lower. "I learned the horrible thing, which is about to happen to this planet, at the hands of those barbarians. The conspiracy is theirs, not mine. They have bribed your Goddess, flattered her and lied to her, coerced her all-powerful goodness to their own evil interests, preparing for the day when they could persuade her to cast your land into the fiery furnace of a ten year drought—"

Somebody in the middle of the court burst out laughing. One by one the natives nudged one another, and booed, and guffawed, until the rising tide of racket drowned out Zeckler's words. "The defendant is obviously lying," roared the prosecutor over the pandemonium. "Any fool knows that the Goddess can't be bribed. How could she be a Goddess if she could?"

Zeckler grew paler. "But—perhaps they were very clever—"

"And how could they flatter her, when she knows, beyond doubt, that she is the most exquisitely radiant creature in all the Universe? And *you* dare to insult her, drag her name in the dirt—"

The hisses grew louder, more belligerent. Cries of "Butcher him!" and "Scald his bowels!" rose from the courtroom. The judge banged for silence, his eyes angry.

"Unless the defendant wishes to take up more of our precious time with these ridiculous lies, the jury—"

"Wait! Your honor, I request a short recess before I present my final plea."

"Recess?"

"A few moments to collect my thoughts, to arrange my case."

The judge settled back with a disgusted snarl. "Do I have to?" he asked Meyerhoff.

Meyerhoff nodded. The judge shrugged, pointing over his shoulder at the little anteroom. "You can go in there," he said,

Somehow, Zeckler managed to stumble from the witness stand, amid riotous boos and hisses, and tottered into the anteroom.

ZECKLER puffed hungrily on a cigarette, and looked up at Meyerhoff with haunted eyes. "It—it doesn't look so good," he muttered.

Meyerhoff's eyes were worried, too. For some reason, he felt a surge of pity and admiration for the haggard little con man. "It's worse than I'd anticipated," he admitted glumly. "That was a good try, but you just don't know enough about them and their Goddess." He sat down wearily. "I don't see what you can do. They want your blood, and they're going to have it. They just won't believe you, no matter *how* big a lie you tell."

Zeckler sat in silence for a moment. "This lying business," he said finally. "Exactly how does it work?"

"The biggest, most convincing liar wins. It's as simple as that. It doesn't matter how outlandish a whopper you tell. Unless, of course, they've made up their minds that you just naturally aren't as big a liar as they are. And it looks like that's just what they've done. It wouldn't make any difference to them *what* you say—unless, somehow, you could *make* them believe it."

Zeckler was on his feet, his eyes suddenly bright with excitement. "Wait a minute," he said tensely. "To tell them a lie that they'd have to believe—a lie they simply couldn't *help* but believe—" He turned on Meyerhoff, his hands trembling. "Do they *think* the way we do—I mean, with logic, cause and effect, examining evidence and drawing conclusions? Given certain evidence, would they have to draw the same conclusion that we have to draw?"

Meyerhoff blinked. "Well—yes. Oh, yes, they're perfectly logical."

Zeckler's eyes flashed, and a huge grin broke out on his sallow face. His thin body fairly shook, and he started hopping up and down on one foot, staring idiotically into space. "If I could only think..." he muttered. "Somebody—somewhere—something I read..."

"Whatever are you talking about?"

"It was a Greek, I think..."

Meyerhoff stared at him. "Oh, come now. Have you gone off your rocker completely? You've got a problem on your hands, man—"

"No, no—I've got a problem in the bag!" Zeckler's cheeks flushed. "Let's go back in there—I think I've got an answer!"

The courtroom quieted the moment they opened the door, and the judge banged the gavel for silence. As soon as Zeckler had taken his seat on the witness stand, the judge turned to the head juryman. "Now, then," he said with happy finality. "The jury—"

"Hold on! Just one minute more."

The judge stared down at Zeckler as if he were a bug on a rock. "Oh, yes. You had something else to say. Well, go ahead and say it."

Zeckler looked sharply around the hushed room. "You want to convict me," he said softly, "in the worst sort of way. Isn't that right?"

The judge looked uncomfortable. "If you've got something to say, go ahead and say it."

"I've got just one statement to make. Short and sweet. But you'd better listen to it, and think it out carefully before you decide that you really want to convict me." He paused, and glanced slyly at the judge. "You don't think much of those who tell the truth, it seems. Well, put *this* statement in your record, then." His voice was loud and clear in the still room. "*All Earthmen are absolutely incapable of telling the truth.*"

Puzzled frowns appeared on the jury's faces. One or two exchanged startled glances, and the room was still as death. The judge stared at him, and then at Meyerhoff, then back. "But you..." he stammered. "You're..." he stopped in mid-sentence, his jaw sagging.

One of the jurymen let out a little squeak, and fainted dead away. It took, all in all, about ten seconds for the statement to soak in.

Then pandemonium broke loose in the courtroom.

REALLY," said Harry Zeckler loftily, "it was so obvious I'm amazed that it didn't occur to me first thing." He settled himself down comfortably in the control cabin of the Interplanetary rocket and grinned at the outline of Altair IV looming larger in the viewscreen.

Paul Meyerhoff stared stonily at the controls, his lips compressed angrily. "You might at least have told me what you were planning."

"And take the chance of being overheard? Don't be silly. It had to come as a bombshell. I had to establish myself as a liar, the prize liar of them all, but I had to tell the sort of lie that they simply could not cope with. Something that would throw them into such utter confusion that they wouldn't *dare* convict me." He grinned impishly at Meyerhoff. "The paradox of Epiminedes the Cretan. It really stopped them cold. They *knew* I was an Earthman, which meant that my statement that Earthmen were liars was a lie, which meant that maybe I wasn't a liar, in which case—oh, it was tailor-made."

"It sure was." Meyerhoff's voice was a snarl.

"Well, it made me out a liar in a class they couldn't approach, didn't it?"

Meyerhoff's face was purple with anger. "Oh, indeed it did! And it put *all* Earthmen in exactly the same class, too."

"So what's honor among thieves? I got off, didn't I?"

Meyerhoff turned on him fiercely. "Oh, you got off just fine. You scared the living daylights out of them. In an eon of lying they never have run up against a short-circuit like that. You've also completely botched any hope of ever setting up a trading alliance with Altair I, and that includes uranium, too. Smart people don't gamble with loaded dice. You scared them so badly they don't want anything to do with us."

Zeckler's grin broadened, and he leaned back luxuriously. "Ah, well. After all, the Trading Alliance was *your* outlook, wasn't it? What a pity." He clucked his tongue sadly. "Me, I've got a fortune in credits sitting back at the consulate waiting for me—enough to keep me on silk for quite a while, I might say. I think I'll just take a nice, long vacation."

Meyerhoff turned to him, and a twinkle of malignant glee appeared in his eyes. "Yes, I think you will. I'm quite sure of it, in fact. Won't cost you a cent, either."

"Eh?"

Meyerhoff grinned unpleasantly. He brushed an imaginary lint fleck from his lapel, and looked up at Zeckler slyly. "That— uh—jury trial. The Altairians weren't any too happy to oblige. They wanted to execute you outright. Thought a trial was awfully silly—until they got their money back, of course. Not too much—just three million credits..."

Zeckler went white. "But that money was in banking custody!"

"Is that right? My goodness. You don't suppose they could have lost those papers, do you?" Meyerhoff grinned at the little con man. "And incidentally, you're under arrest, you know."

A choking sound came from Zeckler's throat. *"Arrest!"*

"Oh, yes. Didn't I tell you? Conspiring to undermine the authority of the Terran Trading Commission. Serious charge, you know. Yes, I think we'll take a nice long vacation together—straight back to Terra. And there I think you'll face a jury trial."

Zeckler sputtered. "There's no evidence! You've got nothing on me! What kind of a frame are you trying to pull?"

"A *lovely* frame. Airtight. A frame from the bottom up, and you're right square in the middle. And this time—" Meyerhoff tapped a cigarette on his thumb with happy finality—"this time I *don't* think you'll get off."

THE END

The Awful Weapon

By ALFRED COPPEL

It was worse than fission bombs, fusion bombs, or any other kind of high explosive!
The object of war is to destroy the enemy's power to resist, as a rule. And that doesn't necessarily entail obliterating the enemy.

THERE WAS no tirade. The Russian delegate was stating facts, and he spoke quietly and with confidence.

"Gentlemen of the Security Council," he said, "there is nothing you can do. The Soviet Union has at long last reached parity with the West in the matter of atomic weapons. For every bomb that you can deliver to a Russian city, we can deliver one in return. No sane man will expect, therefore, to dissuade the Soviet government from its present course by threatening atomic war. For all practical purposes there can be no such thing. Our weapons cancel out. Stalemate—"

He looked across the semi-circular table at the row of grim faces and smiled urbanely.

"You seem disheartened, gentlemen. Believe me, you should be. The West has lost whatever advantage it may once have enjoyed. For every division you can muster, the Soviet can produce five. Our tanks outnumber yours ten to one; our planes twenty to one." He paused for effect and then continued easily. "It is therefore with the greatest pleasure that I—as representative of the Government of the Soviet Union—inform the Security Council that the capitalistic encirclement of the U.S.S.R. is no longer tolerable. Soviet troops will move west within the hour."

The Russian delegate stood waiting for the cries of protest that were bound to come, but the Council room remained strangely silent. Presently, the British delegate rose. "What few British troops are left in western Europe will have orders to offer no resistance," he said, and sat down.

The Russian delegate stared; this was more than he could have hoped for. The French delegate was nodding agreement, and the Danish and Dutch indicating assent.

The American delegate stood up. "Since there are no longer any American forces in Europe," he said, "there can be no resistance to Russian troop movements. What the Russian delegate has said concerning atomic weapons is quite correct. However, the Government of the United States feels it incumbent to warn the Soviet government that there are *other* weapons, and that Soviet forces would do better to remain where they are."

The Russian frowned. "Are you threatening? We, too, have biological weapons, remember. The same stalemate applies to those."

"I was not implying that the United States would indulge in germ warfare," the American delegate said. "I only suggest that the Soviet government restrain its appetite for territory."

The Russian laughed explosively.

"You *suggest?*" He gathered his papers and stuffed them into a bulging briefcase. "With no troops available and only a single squadron of airplane based in England, the United States is in no position to suggest anything. You cannot use atomics or biological weapons; you are quite helpless."

"The United States will resist," the American delegate said quietly.

The Russian did not bother to reply. He jammed his briefcase under his arm and signaled to his staff. Like a squad of infantry, the black-suited delegation stalked out of the meeting room.

The British delegate looked at his American colleague. "This is it, then?"

"Afraid so."

The French delegate shrugged. "I am glad to have it over with at last."

"This weapon...?" The British delegate did not wish to seem overcurious, knowing how touchy Americans could be about security matters, but he really wanted to know.

The American grinned. "An *awful* weapon," he said. "This war will be *hell...*"

THE STRATOSPHERE WAS purple-blue, the stars shining with unnatural brilliance. The flat Asiatic landscape far below was lost in the murk.

The American plane was a fast moving glitter against the static unreality of the sky. Deep within the craft, the radar screen showed the outlines of a Russian city. Leningrad. All over Russia, similar planes were finding other cities. Kiev, Novgorod, Pskov, Moscow.

Fighters were climbing fast into the stratosphere, straining to intercept the tiny invader, but the psychology of stalemate had slowed them down. It was already too late; bomb bay doors were opening in the fleet ship's belly.

Below, in the streets of the city, there was panic. Air-raid sirens screeched; the shelters were jammed with fearful humanity—all cursing the American killers who sought to shatter their city and their lives. Soldiers from the tremendous troop concentrations nearby were trying to maintain a semblance of order, but terror-stricken mobs surged through the ancient streets.

Ten miles above the city, a mechanical brain in a bombsight muttered to itself, analyzing, computing. At last an amber light flashed. Once. Twice. The light turned to red and the airplane surged upward, freed of its load.

Separated from the plane, the bomb arched downward, whistling eerily in the thin air.

Below, horrified radar operators watched the deadly golden speck plunge toward them. Long-forgotten prayers of long-forbidden regions formed on their frozen lips.

The interceptors turned away scattering from the spot where the bomb would strike. The American plane vanished toward the north. All over Russia, American planes were disappearing like the one over Leningrad.

The bomb screamed earthward, twisting and turning. Then, five thousand feet above the teeming streets of the city it exploded with a ridiculous—

Plop!

A few shards of bomb-casing clattered on rooftops and pavements. That was all.

PIETR KALGANIN THEN stumbled out of the suffocating bomb-shelter with pounding heart. It was not the panic of the air raid that had frightened him, nor was it the thick, gloomy darkness of the blacked-out city.

It was the hour that set Pietr Kalganin's hands to trembling. Of course, he told himself, he could blame *some* of the delay on the raid —and possibly his wife might believe him. But she was getting suspicious. And Nadya Petrovna was such a jealous and violent woman! Pietr wondered bleakly why he had ever married her. The very sight of her huge, menacing bulk made his blood run cold with fear.

But soon, he thought excitedly, it would all be over. His nightly meetings with the girl in the apartment downstairs had given him courage; he'd get permission from the party cell to divorce Nadya, and then life would be really worth living again.

He had to be careful, though.

Nadya had a dark mind. Only yesterday she had asked for his factory worker's butter ration, and had flown into a rage when he said he'd lost it. He trembled to think what she might have done if she had known that he'd given it to the girl downstairs...

A strange sort of defiance swept over him as he walked. The night was thick and grimy with the stink of that foolish dud the Americans had dropped. He thought: *Why should I have given my butter to Nadya Petrovna?* The thought of her stuffing her fat face with it made him slightly ill.

The grim, shabby pile where he and Nadya shared a tiny apartment with her brother Mitka and his family materialized out of the gloom and Pietr's feet took him rapidly up the stairs. It would be just in and out tonight again, he thought with anticipation; the girl downstairs was waiting. But his lie would have to be more elaborate than usual in view of the fact that the raid had delayed him. He'd say there was a meeting of the factory party cell. Nadya Petrovna wouldn't dare question that...

On the sixth floor, his door was open; Nadya stood peering around it like a huge, misshapen hawk. The apartment smelled of cabbage and too many people; but except for Nadya, it was quite empty.

"Where is everybody?" he asked.

"Mitka went mad right after the bombing," his wife said. "An MVD man came to check through the building and Mitka told him he thought Comrade Molotov was a fat sausage—"

Pietr wasn't certain he had heard right. "He did *what?*" Mitka had always been a fool, but no one was that big a fool. Pietr decided it must be one of Nadya Petrovna's stupid jokes.

"No," Nadya insisted stolidly. "Mitka called Molotov a sausage and they took him away. Ilyena and the children went down to testify against him."

Pietr Kalganin shook his head. This was all beyond him. *Well,* he thought, *people come and go—I suppose Mitka has gone by this time.*

"I shall be going out again tonight, Nadya Petrovna," he said, "I—" Suddenly he felt peculiar. The lie was on the tip of his tongue, but it was entangled in that odd defiance he had felt walking home. He wanted in that moment to tell the simple truth. He was still talking; he could hear the sound of his own voice babbling, and he listened to it with a detached mixture of shocked horror and perplexed pleasure. "I am going to meet that girl downstairs. You know, the one you're so jealous of—that one. I was late because I was with her before the raid. I like being with her, too. Much better than being with you, Nadya Petrovna."

His wife stared at him in stunned disbelief. Then her huge face began to crinkle. She opened her mouth and released a rending, repulsive sob. "You've gone mad too!" she cried.

"Oh, no, Nadya Petrovna. I'm sane enough. I feel fine. Better than I have in months, in fact." He did, too. That was the strange part of it; he felt like singing.

Nadya began making gurgling sounds in her throat. For one breathless minute, Pietr thought that she might beat him; she was big enough, he told himself with unaccustomed unconcern. But she did not reach for the rolling pin that lay on the cluttered sideboard. She only emitted a catastrophic bellow and stumbled out the door. Pietr stood back and let her by.

He was thinking happily of the girl downstairs as his wife vanished down the musty hallway, still wailing at the top of her voice.

MAJOR VASILI ILYITCH SHAPOSHENKO ran an exasperated hand over his cropped blond hair. His heavy face was twisted into a grimace of absolute and utter frustration.

The tank column was hopelessly stalled. The world, Major Shaposhenko decided, had gone quite mad. Far down the column he could see his second in command engaged in a heated argument with a gunner. Directly under the turret of his own tank, a corporal was snarling invective at a company lieutenant. Everywhere, men were wrangling and voicing the most outlandish opinions.

Colonel Kulin, the regimental commander, had informed Shaposhenko less than one hour before that he personally thought the government was handling this whole stupid war very badly. He had also claimed that at the first opportunity, he was going to report Molotov to the MVD as a saboteur and an incompetent. Shaposhenko had listened with open mouth; he had heard more treason and sheer idiocy given voice in the last few hours than he had heard in the last fifteen years. It had all begun, he told himself, with that asinine dud the Americans dropped on Leningrad.

Shaposhenko shrugged the thought away. It was not his concern. His only duty was to get this infernal tangle of deserted vehicles and quarreling men moving west—

For the next two hours, Shaposhenko slogged through the snow, giving commands with voice and fist. But at the end of that time, there was still no semblance of order. When he demanded compliance to duty, he got long-winded speeches or out-and-out vituperation.

It was beginning to rain. The Major returned to his tank and huddled miserably in the abandoned driver's seat.

Presently, Colonel Kulin arrived out of the rainy greyness. He had a bottle tucked under his arm. He looked very happy.

"Where did you get the vodka?" Shaposhenko demanded testily.

"From the MVD man," the colonel said pleasantly.

Shaposhenko recalled the sour policeman and made several mental reservations about the colonel's veracity—

"You're a liar," he said. His eyes widened; his own voice had said that. Of course, he had thought it for years, but—

Suddenly he smiled. It felt good to call Kulin a liar. Very good, indeed. He did it again. "I've thought you were a liar for years. Rather stupid, too."

Kulin blinked.

"In fact, we've all been liars. I'm tired of it; I'm tired of sitting here in this tin truck. I'm tired of the army and the party and just about everything else."

"That's odd. So am I."

The Major smiled. Perhaps Kulin wasn't as stupid as he thought. He took the bottle from the Colonel and drank thirstily. The vodka tasted good.

"I know a place where there is better vodka even than this," Kulin said. "Schnapps, too. And pink champagne."

Shaposhenko drew a deep breath. "Vienna?"

"Paris."

"Let's go."

The Major's tank roared. It moved out into the rainy afternoon. Soon it was lost to sight, the sound of its exhaust a happy purr fading away in the west. The soldiers of the stalled armored column watched it go disinterestedly and returned to their wrangling.

MARSHAL GORIN AND THE MVD man waited musically on his broad chest. One simply did not divest a Marshal of the Red Army and a Hero of the Soviet Union in a cavalier manner. At least a simple MVD captain didn't.

The Premier would attend to it personally, and so the Marshal and the Captain waited in the vast empty hall at the foot of the ancient Red Stairs.

The Kremlin, Gorin thought with perverse pleasure, was very quiet tonight—in direct contrast to the riots that were surging through the streets of Moscow. Things were really in a pretty mess, he reflected. Desertions in droves from the armed forces; whole villages pulling up stakes and moving west; subordinates being insolent to just about everybody. The country in general, and Moscow in particular, was completely disorganized. Yet few lives had been lost. Here and there a soldier had knifed an officer and a man or woman an unfaithful spouse, but other than that the confusion was bloodless.

One had to admire the devilish cleverness of the Americans, Gorin decided reluctantly. This was their doing. Without firing a single shot, they had made the vast Soviet incapable of aggression. It was rather miraculous.

He looked down at the MVD man. Seemed a decent enough chap, though one could never tell about the MVD. Looked frightened, though. Probably awed, by being ordered to arrest a Marshal. Gorin shook his head sadly. That fat sausage of a Premier! Trying to blame this insane debacle on his military men! Typical politician's reaction. If the army had overrun western Europe on schedule, he would have taken all the credit. Gorin's mouth twitched with disdain. He had never liked the Premier. Hated him, in fact. Despised him.

Shooting people wasn't going to help matters now. But that was the only thing the Premier did really well. What was needed was a little common sense, not corpses... Well, amended Gorin, *one* corpse wouldn't do any harm—not if it were the right one. Then a provisional government and peace with the west. After that, fewer lies and less shooting of people. That was the thing.

He would have to take the Captain into his confidence, he decided. Even an MVD man couldn't make matters any worse. Gorin smiled. And then—as the Premier came down the Red Stairs—

Five minutes later, the government of the U.S.S.R. changed form...

THE room of the U.N. headquarters in New York was dark except for the reflected glow from the telescreen. The assembled members of the Security Council watched and listened to the image on the screen with mixed emotions.

"There is no use going on with this idiotic war," Gorin's image said. "Most of us never wanted it, and now that the authority is in the hands of the Provisional Government, we request your peace terms."

"No terms, Gorin," the Secretary General said.

"You mean you want nothing from us?"

"Only self-determination for the small countries you have taken over directly or indirectly."

"Agreed!" Gorin beamed out of the telescreen.

The American delegate grinned. "And you can't lie, can you Gorin?"

Gorin shook his head. "No, I can't. How did you do it?"

"The bombs contained a high concentrate of a secret scopolamine derivative. A truth serum."

Gorin coughed discretely. "Uh, when will it wear off? It makes certain uh...personal relations rather...uh unconventional, you know."

"I'm afraid you'll have to put up with it for a few months, at least. Once the molecules are dispersed in the air they combine with nitrogen to form a heavy compound. The winds can't blow it away. It will just take time that's all. Meanwhile, no lying. Therefore no police-state. Simple as that."

"This will finish politicians," Gorin said happily.

There was a loud clatter outside the communications room and a panting courier burst through the door. His face was ghastly pale. He drew the American delegate aside and there was a whispered, conference.

Presently the courier rushed out of the room again, leaving the American delegate gaunt and grey-faced. The other delegates gathered about him, all asking questions at once.

He staggered to a chair and sank down into it like an old man. He looked around him bleakly.

"You know the plant at Aberdeen that has been making the scopolamine gas?"

The others nodded.

"It has blown up. Ten storage tanks of fifty million cubic feet—gone! *Dispersed in the atmosphere!*" His voice grew thin. "The wind is pushing it toward...toward Washington." He got to his feet and hobbled for the door, a man suddenly old before his time. He turned to face his colleagues, his haggard face contorted with horror.

"And...Oh, my God...!" He sobbed, *"This is an election year...!"*

THE END

Assassin

By J. F. BONE

The aliens wooed Earth with gifts, love, patience and peace. Who could resist them? After all, no one shoots Santa Claus!

THE RIFLE LAY comfortably in his hands, a gleaming precision instrument that exuded a faint odor of gun oil and powder solvent. It was a perfect specimen of the gunsmith's art, a semi-automatic rifle with a telescopic sight—a precisely engineered tool that could hurl death with pinpoint accuracy for better than half a mile.

Daniel Matson eyed the weapon with bleak gray eyes, the eyes of a hunter framed in the passionless face of an executioner. His blunt hands were steady as they lifted the gun and tried a dry shot at an imaginary target. He nodded to himself. He was ready. Carefully he laid the rifle down on the mattress, which covered the floor of his firing point, and looked out through the hole in the brickwork to the narrow canyon of the street below.

The crowd had thickened. It had been gathering since early morning, and the growing press of spectators had now become solid walls of people lining the street, packed tightly together on the sidewalks. Yet despite the fact that there were virtually no police, the crowd did not overflow into the streets, nor was there any of the pushing crowding impatience that once attended an assemblage of this sort. Instead there was a placid tolerance, a spirit of friendly good will, an ingenuous complaisance that grated on Matson's nerves like the screeching rasp of a file drawn across the edge of thin metal. He shivered uncontrollably. It was hard to be a free man in a world of slaves.

It was a measure of the Aztlan's triumph that only a bare half-dozen police 'copters patrolled the empty skies above the parade route. The aliens had done this—had conquered the world without firing a shot or speaking a word in anger. They had wooed Earth with understanding patience and superlative guile—and Earth had fallen into their hands like a lovesick virgin! There never had been any real opposition, and what there was had been completely ineffective. Most of those who had opposed the aliens were out of circulation, imprisoned in correctional institutions, undergoing rehabilitation. Rehabilitation! A six bit word for dehumanizing. When those poor devils finished their treatment with Aztlan brainwashing techniques, they would be just like these sheep below, with the difference that they would never be able to be anything else. But these other stupid fools crowding the sidewalks, waiting to hail their destruction—these were the ones who must be saved. They—not the martyrs of the underground—were the important part of humanity.

A police 'copter wind-milled slowly down the avenue toward his hiding place, the rotating vanes and insect body of the craft starkly outlined against the jagged backdrop of the city's skyline. He laughed soundlessly as the susurrating flutter of the rotor blades beat overhead and died whispering in the distance down the long canyon of the street. His position had been chosen with care, and was invisible from air and ground alike. He had selected it months ago, and had taken considerable pains to conceal its true purpose. But after today concealment wouldn't matter. If things went as he hoped, the place might someday become a shrine. The idea amused him.

Strange, he mused, how events conspire to change a man's career. Seven years ago he had been a respected and important member of that far different sort of crowd, which had welcomed the visitors from space. That was a human crowd—half afraid, wholly curious, jostling, noisy, pushing—a teeming swarm that clustered in a thick disorderly ring around the silver disc that lay in the center of the International Airport overlooking Puget Sound. Then—he could have predicted his career. And none of the predictions would have been true—for none included a man with a rifle waiting in a blind for the game to approach within range...

The Aztlan ship had landed early that July morning, dropping silently through the overcast covering International Airport. It settled gently to rest precisely in the center of the junction of the three main runways of the field, effectively tying up the transcontinental and transoceanic traffic. Fully five hundred feet in diameter, the giant ship squatted massively on the runway junction, cracking and buckling the thick concrete runways under its enormous weight.

By noon, after the first skepticism had died, and the unbelievable TV pictures had been flashed to their waiting audience, the crowd began to gather. All through that hot July morning they came, increasing by the minute as farther outlying districts poured their curious into the Airport. By early afternoon, literally hundreds of millions of eyes were watching the great ship over a worldwide network of television stations, which cancelled their regular programs to give their viewers an uninterrupted view of the enigmatic craft.

By mid-morning the sun had burned off the overcast and was shining with brassy brilliance upon the squads of sweating soldiers from Fort Lewis, and more sweating squads of blue-clad police from the metropolitan area of Seattle-Tacoma. The police and soldiery quickly formed a ring around the ship and cleared a narrow lane around the periphery, and this they maintained despite the increasing pressure of the crowd.

The hours passed and nothing happened. The faint creaking and snapping sounds as the seamless hull of the vessel warmed its space-chilled metal in the warmth of the summer sun were lost in the growing impatience of the crowd. They wanted something to happen. Shouts and catcalls filled the air as more nervous individuals clamored to relieve the tension. Off to one side a small group began to clap their hands rhythmically. The little claque gained recruits, and within moments the air was riven by the thunder of thousands of palms meeting in unison. Frightened the crowd might be, but greater than fear was the desire to see what sort of creatures were inside.

Matson stood in the cleared area surrounding the ship, a position of privilege he shared with a few city and state officials and the high brass from McChord Field, Fort Lewis, and Bremerton Navy Yard. He was one of the bright young men who had chosen Government Service as a career, and who, in these days of science-consciousness had risen rapidly through ability and merit promotions to become the Director of the Office of Scientific Research while still in his early thirties. A dedicated man, trained in the bitter school of ideological survival, he understood what the alien science could mean to this world. Their knowledge would secure peace in whatever terms the possessors cared to name, and Matson intended to make sure that his nation was the one which possessed that knowledge.

He stood beside a tall scholarly looking man named Roger Thornton, who was his friend and incidentally the Commissioner of Police for the Twin City metropolitan area. To a casual eye, their positions should be reversed, for the lean ascetic Thornton looked far more like the accepted idea of a scientist than burly, thick shouldered, square faced Matson, whose every movement shouted *Cop*.

Matson glanced quizzically at the taller man. "Well, Roger, I wonder how long those birds inside are going to keep us waiting before we get a look at then?"

"You'd be surprised if they really were birds, wouldn't you?" Thornton asked with a faint smile. "But seriously, I hope it isn't too much longer. This mob is giving the boys a bad time." He looked anxiously at the strained line of police and soldiery. "I guess I should have ordered out the night shift and reserves instead of just the riot squad. From the looks of things they'll be needed if this crowd gets any more unruly."

Matson chuckled. "You're an alarmist," he said mildly. "As far as I can see they're doing all right. I'm not worried about them— or the crowd, for that matter. The thing that's bothering me is my feet. I've been standing on 'em for six hours and they're *killing* me."

"Mine too," Thornton sighed. "Tell you what I'll do. When this is all over I'll split a bucket of hot water and a pint of arnica with you."

"It's a deal," Matson said.

As he spoke a deep musical hum came from inside the ship, and a section of the rim beside him separated along invisible lines of juncture, swinging downward to form a broad ramp leading upward to a square orifice in the rim of the ship. A bright shadowless light that seemed to come from the metal walls of the opening framed the shape of the star traveler who stood there, rigidly erect, looking over the heads of the section of the crowd before him.

A concerted gasp of awe and admiration rose from the crowd—a gasp that was echoed throughout the entire ring that surrounded the ship. There must be other openings like this one, Matson thought dully as he stared at the being from space. Behind him an Army tank rumbled noisily on its treads as it drove through the crowd toward the ship, the long gun in its turret lifting like an alert finger to point at the figure of the alien.

The stranger didn't move from his unnaturally stiff position. His oddly luminous eyes never wavered from their fixed stare at a point far beyond the outermost fringes of the crowd. Seven feet tall, obviously masculine, he differed from mankind only in minor details. His long slender hands lacked the little finger, and his waist was abnormally small. Other than that, he was human in external appearance. A wide sleeved tunic of metallic fabric covered his upper body, gathered in at his narrow waist by a broad metal belt studded with tiny bosses. The tunic ended halfway between hip and knee, revealing powerfully muscled legs encased in silvery hose. Bright yellow hair hung to his shoulders, clipped short in a square bang across his forehead. His face was long, clean featured and extraordinarily calm—almost godlike in its repose. Matson stared, fascinated. He had the curious impression that the visitor had stepped bodily out of the Middle Ages. His dress and haircut were almost identical with that of a medieval courtier.

The star man raised his hand—his strangely luminous steel gray eyes scanned the crowd—and into Matson's mind came a wave of peaceful calm, a warm feeling of goodwill and brotherhood, an indescribable feeling of soothing relaxation. With an odd sense of shock Matson realized that he was not the only one to experience this. As far back as the farthest hangers-on near the airport gates the tenseness of the waiting crowd relaxed. The effect was amazing! Troops lowered their weapons with shamefaced smiles on their faces. Police relaxed their sweating vigilance. The crowd stirred, moving backward to give its members room. The emotion-charged atmosphere vanished as though it had never been. And a cold chill played icy fingers up the spine of Daniel Matson. He had felt the full impact of the alien's projection, and he was more frightened than he had ever been in his life...

THEY HAD BEEN clever—damnably clever! That initial greeting with its disarming undertones of empathy and innocence had accomplished its purpose. It had emasculated Mankind's natural suspicion of strangers. And their subsequent actions—so beautifully timed—so careful to avoid the slightest hint of evil, had completed what their magnificently staged appearance had begun.

The feeling of trust had persisted. It lasted through quarantine, clearance, the public receptions, and the private meetings with scientists and the heads of government. It had persisted unabated through the entire two months they remained in the Twin City area. The aliens remained as they had been in the beginning—completely unspoiled by the interest shown in them. They remained simple, unaffected, and friendly, displaying an ingenuous innocence that demanded a corresponding faith in return.

Most of their time was spent at the University of Washington, where at their own request they were studied by curious scholars, and in return were given courses in human history and behavior. They were quite frank about their reasons for following such a course of action—according to their spokesman Ixtl they wanted to learn human ways in order to make a better impression when they visited the rest of Mankind. Matson read that blurb in an official press release and laughed cynically. Better impression, hah! They couldn't have done any better if they had an entire corps of public relations specialists assisting them! They struck exactly the right note—and how could they improve on perfection?

From the beginning they left their great ship open and unguarded while they commuted back and forth from the airport to the campus. And naturally the government quickly rectified the second error and took instant advantage of the first. A guard was posted around the ship to keep it clear of the unofficially curious, while the officially curious combed the vessel's interior with a fine-tooth comb. Teams of scientists and technicians under Matson's direction swarmed through the ship, searching with the most advanced methods of human science for the secrets of the aliens.

They quickly discovered that while the star travelers might be trusting, they were not exactly fools. There was nothing about the impenetrably shielded mechanisms that gave the slightest clue as to their purpose or to the principles upon which they operated—nor were there any visible controls. The ship was as blankly uncommunicative as a brick wall.

Matson was annoyed. He had expected more than this, and his frustration drove him to watch the aliens closely. He followed them, sat in on their sessions with the scholars at the University, watched them at their frequent public appearances, and came to know them well enough to recognize the microscopic differences that made them individuals. To the casual eye they were as alike as peas in a pod, but Matson could separate Farn from Quicha, and Laz from Acana—and Ixtl—well he would have stood out from the others in any circumstances. But Matson never intruded. He was content to sit in the background and observe.

And what he saw bothered him.

They gave him no reason for their appearance on Earth, and whenever the question came up Ixtl parried it adroitly. They were obviously not explorers for they displayed a startling familiarity with Earth's geography and ecology. They were possibly ambassadors, although they behaved like no ambassadors he had ever seen. They might be traders, although what they would trade only God and the aliens knew—and neither party was in a talking mood. Mysteries bothered Matson. He didn't like them. But they could keep their mystery if he could only have the technical knowledge that was concealed beneath their beautifully shaped skulls.

At that, he had to admit that their appearance had come at precisely the right time. No one better than he knew how close Mankind had been to the final war, when the last two major antagonists on Earth were girding their human and industrial power for a final showdown. But the aliens had become a diversion. The impending war was forgotten while men waited to see what was coming next. It was obvious that the star men had a reason for being here, and until they chose to reveal it, humanity would forget its deadly problems in anticipation of the answer to this delightful puzzle that had come to them from outer space.

Matson was thankful for the breathing space, all too well aware that it might be the last that Mankind might have, but the enigma of the aliens still bothered him.

He was walking down the main corridor of the Physics Building on the University campus, wondering as he constantly did about how he could extract some useful knowledge from the aliens when a quiet voice speaking accentless English sounded behind him.

"What precisely do you wish to know, Dr. Matson?" the voice said.

Matson whirled to face the questioner, and looked into the face of Ixtl. The alien was smiling, apparently pleased at having startled him. "What gave you the idea that I wanted to know anything?" he asked.

"You did," Ixtl said. "We all have been conscious of your thoughts for many days. Forgive me for intruding, but I must. Your speculations radiate on such a broad band that we cannot help being aware of them. It has been quite difficult for us to study your customs and history with this high-level background noise. We are aware of your interest, but your thoughts are so confused that we have never found questions we could answer. If you would be more specific we would be happy to give you the information which you seek."

"Oh yeah," Matson thought.

"Of course. It would be to our advantage to have your disturbing speculations satisfied and your fears set at rest. We could accomplish more in a calmer environment. It is too bad that you do not receive as strongly as you transmit. If you did, direct mental contact would convince you that our reasons for satisfying you are good. But you need not fear us, Earthman. We intend you no harm. Indeed, we plan to help you once we learn enough to formulate a proper program."

"I do not fear you," Matson said—knowing that he lied.

"Perhaps not consciously," Ixtl said graciously, "but nevertheless fear is in you. It is too bad—and besides," he continued with a faint smile "it is very uncomfortable. Your glandular emotions are quite primitive, and very disturbing."

"I'll try to keep them under control," Matson said dryly.

"Physical control is not enough. With you there would have to be mental control as well. Unfortunately you radiate much more strongly than your fellow men, and we are unable to shut you out without exerting considerable effort that could better be employed elsewhere." The alien eyed Matson speculatively. "There you go again," he said. "Now you're angry."

Matson tried to force his mind to utter blankness, and the alien smiled at him. "It does some good—but not much," he said. "Conscious control is never perfect."

"Well then, what can I do?"

"Go away. Your range fortunately is short."

Matson looked at the alien. "Not yet," he said coldly. "I'm still looking for something."

"Our technology," Ixtl nodded. "I know. However I can assure you it will be of no help to you. You simply do not have the necessary background. Our science is based upon a completely different philosophy from yours."

To Matson the terms were contradictory.

"Not as much as you think," Ixtl continued imperturbably. "As you will find out, I was speaking quite precisely." He paused and eyed Matson thoughtfully. "It seems as though the only way to remove your disturbing presence is to show you that our technology is of no help to you. I will make a bargain with you. We shall show you our machines, and in return you will stop harassing us. We will do all in our power to make you understand; but whether you do or do not, you will promise to leave and allow us to continue our studies in peace. Is that agreeable?"

Matson swallowed the lump in his throat. Here it was—handed to him on a silver platter—and suddenly he wasn't sure that he wanted it!

"It is," he said. After all, it was all he could expect.

They met that night at the spaceship. The aliens, tall, calm and cool; Matson stocky, heavy-set and sweating. The contrast was infernally sharp, Matson thought. It was as if a primitive savage were meeting a group of nuclear physicists at Los Alamos. For some unknown reason he felt ashamed that he had forced these people to his wishes. But the aliens were pleasant about it. They took the imposition in their usual friendly way.

"Now," Ixtl said, "exactly what do you want to see—to know?"

"First of all, what is the principle of your space drive?"

"There are two," the alien said. "The drive that moves this ship in normal space time is derived from Lurgil's Fourth Order equations concerning the release of subatomic energy in a restricted space time continuum. Now don't protest! I know you know nothing of Lurgil, nor of Fourth Order equations. And while I can show you the mathematics, I'm afraid they will be of little help. You see, our Fourth Order is based upon a process that you would call Psychomathematics and that is something I am sure you have not yet achieved."

Matson shook his head. "I never heard of it," he admitted.

"The second drive operates in warped space time," Ixtl continued, "hyperspace in your language, and its theory is much more difficult than that of our normal drive, although its application is quite simple, merely involving apposition of congruent surfaces of hyper and normal space at stress points in the ether where high gravitational fields balance. Navigation in hyperspace is done by electronic computer—somewhat more advanced models than yours. However, I can't give you the basis behind the hyperspace drive." Ixtl smiled depreciatingly. "You see, I don't know them myself. Only a few of the most advanced minds of Aztlan can understand. We merely operate the machines."

Matson shrugged. He had expected something like this. Now they would stall him off about the machines after handing him a fast line of double-talk.

"As I said," Ixtl went on, "there is no basis for understanding. Still, if it will satisfy you, we will show you our machines—and the mathematics that created them although I doubt that you will learn anything more from them than you have from our explanation."

"I could try," Matson said grimly.

"Very well," Ixtl replied.

He led the way into the center of the ship where the seamless housings stood, the housings that had baffled some of the better minds of Earth. Matson watched while the star men proceeded to be helpful. The housings fell apart at invisible lines of juncture, revealing mechanisms of baffling simplicity, and some things that didn't look like machines at all. The aliens stripped the strange devices and Ixtl attempted to explain. They had antigravity, force fields, faster than light drive, and advanced design computers that could be packed in a suitcase. There were weird devices whose components seemed to run out of sight at crazily impossible angles, other things that rotated frictionlessly, suspended in fields of pure force, and still others, which his mind could not envisage even after his eyes had seen them. All about him lay the evidence of a science so advanced and alien that his brain shrank from the sight, refusing to believe such things existed. And their math was worse! It began where Einstein left off and went off at an incomprehensible tangent that involved psychology and ESP. Matson was lost after the first five seconds.

Stunned, uncomprehending and deflated, he left the ship. An impression that he was standing with his toe barely inside the door of knowledge became a conscious certainty as he walked slowly to his car. The wry thought crossed his mind that if the aliens were trying to convince him of his abysmal ignorance, they had succeeded far beyond their fondest dreams!

They certainly had, Matson thought grimly as he selected five cartridges from the box lying beside him. In fact they had succeeded too well. They had turned his deflation into antagonism, his ignorance into distrust. Like a savage, he suspected what he could not understand. But unlike the true primitive, the emotional distrust didn't interfere with his ability to reason or to draw logical inferences from the data which he accumulated. In attempting to convince, Ixtl had oversold his case.

IT WAS SHORTLY after he had returned to Washington that the aliens gave the waiting world the reasons for their appearance on Earth. They were, they said, members of a very ancient highly evolved culture called Aztlan. And the Aztlans, long past the need for conquest and expansion, had turned their mighty science to the help of other, less fortunate, races in the galaxy. The aliens were, in a sense, missionaries—one of hundreds of teams travelling the star lanes to bring the benefits of Aztlan culture to less favored worlds.

They were, they unblushingly admitted, altruists—interested only in helping others.

It was pure corn, Matson reflected cynically, but the world lapped it up and howled for more. After decades of cold war, luke-warm war, and sporadic outbreaks of violence that were inevitably building to atomic destruction, men were willing to try anything that would ease the continual burden of strain and worry. To Mankind, the Aztlans' words were as refreshing as a cool breeze of hope in a desert of despair.

And the world got what it wanted.

Quite suddenly the aliens left the Northwest, and accompanied by protective squads of FBI and Secret Service began to cross the nation. Taking widely separated paths they visited cities, towns, and farms, exhibiting the greatest curiosity about the workings of human civilization. And, in turn, they were examined by hordes of hopeful humans. Everywhere they went, they spread their message of good will and hope backed by the incredibly convincing power of their telepathic minds. Behind them, they left peace and hopeful calm—before them, anticipation mounted. It rose to a crescendo in New York where the paths of the star men met.

The Aztlans invaded the United Nations. They spoke to the General Assembly and the Security Council, were interviewed by the secretariat and reporters from a hundred foreign lands. They told their story with such conviction that even the Communist bloc failed to raise an objection, which was as amazing to the majority of the delegates as the fact of the star men themselves. Altruism, it seemed had no conflict with dialectic materialism. The aliens offered a watered-down variety of their technology to the peoples of Earth with no strings attached, and the governments of Earth accepted with open hands, much as a small boy accepts a cookie from his mother. It was impossible for men to resist the lure of something for nothing, particularly when it was offered by such people as the Aztlans. After all, Matson reflected bitterly, nobody shoots Santa Claus!

From every nation in the world came invitations to the aliens to visit their lands. The star men cheerfully accepted. They moved across Europe, Asia, and Africa—visited South America, Central

America, the Middle East and Oceania. No country escaped them. They absorbed languages, learned customs, and spread good will. Everywhere they went relaxation followed in their footsteps and throughout the world arose a realization of the essential brotherhood of man.

It took nearly three years of continual travelling before the aliens again assembled at U.N. headquarters to begin the second part of their promised plan—to give their science to Earth. And men waited with calm expectation for the dawn of Golden Age.

Matson's lips twisted. Fools! Blind, stupid fools! Selling their birthright for a mess of pottage! He shifted the rifle across his knees and began filling the magazine with cartridges. He felt an empty loneliness as he closed the action over the filled magazine and turned the safety to "on." There was no comforting knowledge of support and sympathy to sustain him in what he was about to do. There was no real hope that there ever would be. His was a voice crying in the wilderness, a voice that was ignored—as it had been when he visited the President of the United States...

MATSON entered the White House, presented his appointment card, and was ushered past ice-eyed Secret Service men into the presidential office. It was as close as he had ever been to the Chief Executive, and he stared with polite curiosity across the width of desk that separated them.

"I wanted to see you about the Aztlan business," the President began without preamble. "You were there when their ship landed, and you are also one of the few men in the country who has seen them alone. In addition, your office will probably be handling the bulk of our requests in regard to the offer they made yesterday in the U.N. You're in a favorable spot." The President smiled and shrugged. "I wanted to talk with you sooner, but business and routine play the devil with one's desires in this office.

"Now tell me," he continued, "your impression of these people."

"They're an enigma," Matson said flatly. "To tell the truth, I can't figure them out." He ran his fingers through his hair with a worried gesture. "I'm supposed to be a pretty fair physicist, and I've had quite a bit of training in the social sciences, but both the mechanisms and the psychology of these Aztlans are beyond my comprehension. All I can say for sure is that they're as far beyond us as we are beyond the cavemen. In fact, we have so little in common that I can't think of a single reason why they would want to stay here, and the fact that they do only adds to my confusion."

"But you must have learned something," the President said.

"Oh, we've managed to collect data," Matson replied. "But there's a lot of difference between data and knowledge."

"I can appreciate that, but I'd still like to know what you think. Your opinion could have some weight."

Matson doubted it. His opinions were contrary to those of the majority. Still, the Chief asked for it—and he might possibly have an open mind. It was a chance worth taking.

"Well, Sir, I suppose you've heard of the so-called "wild talents" some of our own people occasionally possess?"

The President nodded.

"It is my belief," Matson continued, "that the Aztlans possess these to a far greater degree than we do, and that their science is based upon them. They have something, which they call psychomathematics, which by definition is the mathematics of the mind, and this seems to be the basis of their physical science. I saw their machines, and I must confess that their purpose baffled me until I realized that they must be mechanisms for amplifying their own natural equipment. We know little or nothing about psi phenomena, so it is no wonder I couldn't figure them out. As a matter of fact we've always treated psi as something that shouldn't be mentioned in polite scientific conversation."

The President grinned. "I always thought you boys had your blind spots."

"We do—but when we're confronted with a fact, we try to find out something about it—that is if the fact hits us hard enough, often enough."

"Well, you've been hit hard and often," the President chuckled. "What did you find out?"

"Facts," Matson said grimly, "just facts. Things that could be determined by observation and measurement. We know that the aliens are telepathic. We also know that they have a form of ESP—or perhaps a recognition of danger would be a better term—

and we know its range is somewhat over a third of a mile. We know that they're telekinetic. The lack of visible controls in their ship would tell us that, even if we hadn't seen them move small objects at a distance. We know that they have eidetic memories, and that they can reason on an extremely high level. Other than that we know nothing. We don't even know their physical structure. We've tried X-ray but they're radio-opaque. We've tried using some human sensitives from the Rhine Institute, but they're unable to get anywhere. They just turn empathic in the aliens' presence, and when we get them back, they do nothing but babble about the beauty of the Aztlan soul."

"Considering the difficulties, you haven't done too badly," the President said. "I take it then, that you're convinced that they are an advanced life form. But do you think they're sincere in their attitude toward us?"

"Oh, they're sincere enough," Matson said. "The only trouble is that we don't know just what they're sincere about. You see, sir, we are in the position of a savage to whom a trader brings the luxuries of civilization. To the savage, the trader may represent purest altruism, giving away such valuable things as glass beads and machine made cloth for useless pieces of yellow rock and the skins of some native pest. The savage hasn't the slightest inkling that he's being exploited. By the time he realizes he's been had, and the yellow rock is gold and the skins are mink, he has become so dependent upon the goods for which the trader has whetted his appetite that he inevitably becomes an economic slave.

"Of course you can argue that the cloth and beads are far more valuable to the savage than the gold or mink. But in the last analysis, value is determined by the higher culture, and by that standard, the savage gets taken. And ultimately civilization moves in and the superior culture of the trader's race determines how the savage will act.

"Still, the savage has a basis for his acts. He is giving something for something—making a trade. But we're not even in that position. The aliens apparently want nothing from us. They have asked for nothing except our good will, and that isn't a tradable item."

"But they're altruists," the President protested.

"Sir, do you think that they're insane?" Matson asked curiously. "Do they appear like fanatics to you?"

"But we can't apply our standards to them. You yourself have said that their civilization is more advanced than ours."

"Whose standards can we apply?" Matson asked. "If not ours, then whose? The only standards that we can possibly apply are our own, and in the entire history of human experience there has never been a single culture that has had a basis of pure altruism. Such a culture could not possibly exist. It would be overrun and gobbled up by its practical neighbors before it drew its first breath.

"We must assume that the culture from which these aliens come has had a practical basis in its evolutionary history. It could not have risen full blown and altruistic like Minerva from the brain of Jove. And if the culture had a practical basis in the past, it logically follows that it has a practical basis in the present. Such a survival trait as practicality would probably never be lost no matter how far the Aztlan race has evolved. Therefore, we must concede that they are practical people—people who do not give away something for nothing. But the question still remains—what do they want?

"Whatever it is, I don't think it is anything from which we will profit. No matter how good it looks, I am convinced that cooperation with these aliens will not ultimately be to our advantage. Despite the reports of every investigative agency in this government, I cannot believe that any such thing as pure altruism exists in a sane mind. And whatever I may believe about the Aztlans, I do not think they're insane."

The President sighed. "You are a suspicious man, Matson, and perhaps you are right; but it doesn't matter what you believe—or what I believe for that matter. This government has decided to accept the help the Aztlans are so graciously offering. And until the reverse is proven, we must accept the fact that the star men *are* altruists, and work with them on that basis. You will organize your office along those lines, and extract every gram of information that you can. Even you must admit that they have knowledge that will improve our American way of life."

Matson shook his head doggedly. "I'm afraid, Sir, if you expect Aztlan science to improve the American way of life, you are going to be disappointed. It might promote an Aztlan way of life, but the reverse is hardly possible."

"It's not my decision," the President said. "My hands are tied. Congress voted for the deal by acclamation early this morning. I couldn't veto it even if I wanted to."

"I cannot cooperate in what I believe is our destruction," Matson said in a flat voice.

"Then you have only one course," the President said. "I will be forced to accept your resignation." He sighed wearily. "Personally, I think you're making a mistake. Think it over before you decide. You're a good man, and Lord knows the government can use good men. There are far too many fools in politics." He shrugged and stood up. The interview was over.

Matson returned to his offices, filled with cold frustration. Even the President believed he could do nothing, and these shortsighted politicians who could see nothing more than the immediate gains—there was a special hell reserved for them. There were too many fools in politics. However, he would do what he could. His sense of duty was stronger than his resentment. He would stay on and try to cushion some of the damage, which the Aztlans would inevitably cause, no matter how innocent their motives. And perhaps the President was right—perhaps the alien science would bring more good than harm.

FOR THE NEXT two years Matson watched the spread of Aztlan ideas throughout the world. He saw Aztlan devices bring health, food and shelter to millions in underprivileged countries, and improve the lot of those in more favored nations. He watched tyrannies and authoritarian governments fall under the passive resistance of their peoples. He saw militarism crumble to impotence as the Aztlan influence spread through every facet of society, first as a trickle, then as a steady stream, and finally as a rushing torrent. He saw Mankind on the brink of a Golden Age— and he was unsatisfied.

Reason said that the star men were exactly what they claimed to be. Their every action proved it. Their consistency was perfect, their motives unimpeachable, and the results of their efforts were astounding. Life on Earth was becoming pleasant for millions who never knew the meaning of the word. Living standards improved, and everywhere men were conscious of a feeling of warmth and brotherhood. There was no question that the aliens were doing exactly what they promised.

But reason also told him that the aliens were subtly and methodically destroying everything that man had created, turning him from an individual into a satisfied puppet operated by Aztlan strings. For man is essentially lazy—always searching for the easier way. Why should he struggle to find an answer when the Aztlans had discovered it millennia ago and were perfectly willing to share their knowledge? Why should he use inept human devices when those of the aliens performed similar operations with infinitely more ease and efficiency? Why should he work when all he had to do was ask? There was plan behind their acts.

But at that point reason dissolved into pure speculation. Why were they doing this? Was it merely mistaken kindliness or was there a deeper more subtle motive? Matson didn't know, and in that lack of knowledge lay the hell in which he struggled.

For two years he stayed on with the OSR, watching humanity rush down an unmarked road to an uncertain future. Then he ran away. He could take no more of this blind dependence upon alien wisdom. And with the change in administration that had occurred in the fall elections he no longer had the sense of personal loyalty to the President, which had kept him working at a job he despised. He wanted no part of this brave new world the aliens were creating. He wanted to be alone. Like a hermit of ancient times who abandoned society to seek his soul, Matson fled to the desert country of the Southwest—as far as possible from the Aztlans and their works.

The grimly beautiful land toughened his muscles, blackened his skin, and brought him a measure of peace. Humanity retreated to remoteness except for Seth Winters, a leathery old-timer he had met on his first trip into the desert. The acquaintance had ripened to friendship. Seth furnished a knowledge of the desert country, which Matson lacked, and Matson's money provided the occasional grubstake they needed. For weeks at a time they never saw another human—and Matson was satisfied. The world could go its own way. He would go his.

Running away was the smartest thing he could have done. Others more brave perhaps, or perhaps less rational—had tried to fight, to form an underground movement to oppose these altruists from space; but they were a tiny minority so divided in motives and purpose that they could not act as a unit. They were never more than a nuisance, and without popular support they never had a chance. After the failure of a complicated plot to assassinate the aliens, they were quickly rounded up and confined. And the aliens continued their work.

Matson shrugged. It was funny how little things could mark mileposts in a man's life. If he had known of the underground he probably would have joined it and suffered the same penalty for failure. If he hadn't fled, if he hadn't met Seth Winters, if he hadn't taken that last trip into the desert, if any one of a hundred little things had happened differently he would not be here. That last trip into the desert—he remembered it as though it were yesterday...

The yellow flare of a greasewood fire cast flickering spears of light into the encircling darkness. Above, in the purplish black vault of the moonless sky the stars shone down with icy splendor. The air was quiet, the evening breeze had died, and the stillness of the desert night pressed softly upon the earth. Far away, muted by distance, came the ululating wail of a coyote.

Seth Winters laid another stick of quick-burning greasewood on the fire and squinted across the smoke at Matson who was lying on his back, arms crossed behind his head, eyeing the night sky with the fascination of a dreamer.

"It's certainly peaceful out here," Matson murmured as he rose to his feet, stretched, and sat down again looking into the tiny fire.

"'Tain't nothin' unusual, Dan'l. Not out here it ain't. It's been plumb peaceful on this here desert nigh onto a million years. An' why's it peaceful? Mainly 'cuz there ain't too many humans messin' around in it."

"Possibly you're right, Seth."

"Shore I'm right. It jest ain't nacheral fer a bunch of Homo saps to get together without an argyment startin' somewhere.

'Tain't the nature of the critter to be peaceable. An' y'know, thers the part of this here sweetness an' light between nations that bothers me. Last time I was in Prescott, I set down an' read six months of newspapers—an' everything's jest too damn good to be true. Seems like everybody's gettin' to love everybody else." He shook his head. "The hull world's as sticky-sweet as molasses candy. It jest ain't nacheral!"

"The star men are keeping their word. They said that they would bring us peace. Isn't that what they're doing?"

"Shucks Dan'l—that don't give 'em no call to make the world a blasted honey-pot with everybody bubblin' over with brotherly love. There ain't no real excitement left. Even the Commies ain't raisin' hell like they useta. People are gettin' more like a bunch of damn woolies every day."

"I'll admit that Mankind had herd instincts," Matson replied lazily, "but I've never thought of them as particularly sheeplike. More like a wolf pack, I'd say."

"Wal, there's nothin' wolflike about 'em right now. Look, Dan'l, yuh know what a wolf pack's like. They're smart, tough, and mean—an' the old boss wolf is the smartest, toughest, and meanest critter in the hull pack. The others respect him 'cuz he's proved his ability to lead. But take a sheep flock now—the bellwether is jest a nice gentle old castrate thet'll do jest whut the sheepherder wants. He's got no originality. He's jest a noise thet the rest faller."

"Could be."

"It shore is! Jes fr instance, an' speakin' of bellwethers, have yuh ever heard of a character called Throckmorton Bixbee?"

"Can't say I have. He sounds like a nance."

"Whutever a nance is—he's it! But yuh're talkin' about our next President, unless all the prophets are wrong. He's jest as bad as his name. Of all the gutless wonders I've ever heard of that pilgrim takes the prize. He even *looks* like a rabbit."

"I can see where I had better catch up on some contemporary history," Matson said. "I've been out in the sticks too long."

"If yuh know what's good fer yuh, yuh'll stay here. The rest of the country's goin' t'hell. Brother Bixbee's jest a sample. About the only thing that'd recommend him is that he's hot fer peace— an' he's got those furriners' blessing. Seems like those freaks swing a lotta weight nowadays, an' they ain't shy about tellin' folks who an' what they favor. They've got bold as brass this past year."

Matson nodded idly—then stiffened—turning a wide-eyed stare on Seth. A blinding light exploded in his brain as the words sank in. With crystal clarity he knew the answer! He laughed harshly.

Winters stared at him with mild surprise. "What's bit yuh, Dan'l?"

But Matson was completely oblivious, busily buttressing the flash of inspiration. Sure—that was the only thing it *could* be. Those aliens were working on a program—one that was grimly recognizable once his attention was focused on it. There must have been considerable pressure to make them move so fast that a short-lived human could see what they were planning—but Matson had a good idea of what was driving them, an atomic war that could decimate the world would be all the spur they'd need!

They weren't playing for penny ante stakes. They didn't want to exploit Mankind. They didn't give a *damn* about Mankind. To them humanity was merely an unavoidable nuisance—something to be pushed aside, to be made harmless and dependent, and ultimately to be quietly and bloodlessly eliminated. Man's civilization held nothing that the star men wanted, but man's planet—that was a different story! Truly the aliens were right when they considered man a savage. Like the savage, man didn't realize his most valuable possession was his land!

The peaceful penetration was what had fooled him. Mankind, faced with a similar situation, and working from a position of overwhelming strength would have reacted differently. Humanity would have invaded and conquered. But the aliens had not even considered this obvious step.

Why?

The answer was simple and logical. They couldn't! Even though their technology was advanced enough to exterminate man with little or no loss to themselves, combat and slaughter must be repulsive to them. It had to be. With their telepathic minds they would necessarily have a pathologic horror of suffering. They were so highly evolved that they simply couldn't fight—at least not with the weapons of humanity. But they could use the subtler weapon of altruism.

And even more important—uncontrolled emotions were poison to them. In fact Ixtl had admitted it back in Seattle. The primitive psi waves of humanity's hates, lusts, fears, and exaltations must be unbearable torture to a race long past such animal outbursts. That was—must be—why they were moving so fast. For their own safety, emotion had to be damped out of the human race.

Matson had a faint conception of what the aliens must have suffered when they first surveyed that crowd at International Airport. No wonder they looked so strangely immobile at that first contact… The raw emotion must have nearly killed them. He felt a reluctant sort of admiration for their courage, for the dedicated bravery needed to face that crowd and establish a beachhead of tranquility. Those first few minutes must have had compressed in them the agonies of a lifetime!

Matson grinned coldly. The aliens were not invulnerable. If Mankind could be taught to fear and hate them, and if that emotion could be focussed, they never again would try to take this world. It would be sheer suicide. As long as Mankind kept its emotions it would be safe from this sort of invasion. But the problem was to teach Mankind to fear and hate. Shock would do it, but how could that shock be applied?

The thought led inevitably to the only possible conclusion. The aliens would have to be killed, and in such a manner as to make humanity fear retaliation from the stars. Fear would unite men against a possible invasion, and fear would force men to reach for the stars to forestall retribution.

Matson grinned thinly. Human nature couldn't have changed much these past years. Even with master psychologists like the Aztlans operating upon it, changes in emotional pattern would require generations. He sighed, looked into the anxious face of Seth Winters, and returned to the reality of the desert night. His course was set. He knew what he had to do.

HE LAID THE rifle across his knees and opened the little leather box sewn to the side of the gun case. With precise, careful movements he removed the silencer and fitted it to the threaded muzzle of the gun. The bulky, blue excrescence changed the rifle from a thing of beauty to one of murder. He looked at it distastefully, then shrugged and stretched out on the mattress, easing the ugly muzzle through the hole in the brickwork. It wouldn't be long now...

He glanced upward through the window above him at the Weather Bureau instruments atop a nearby building. The metal cups of the anemometer hung motionless against the metallic blue of the sky. No wind stirred in the deep canyons of the city streets as the sun climbed in blazing splendor above the towering buildings. He moved a trifle, shifting the muzzle of the gun until it bore upon the sidewalks. The telescopic sight picked out faces from the waiting crowd with a crystal clarity. Everywhere was the same sheep-like placidity. He shuddered, the sights jumping crazily from one face to another, wondering if he had misjudged his race, if he had really come too late, if he had underestimated the powers of the Aztlans.

Far down the avenue, an excited hum came to his ears, and the watching crowd stirred. Faces lighted and Matson sighed. He was not wrong. Emotion was only suppressed, not vanished. There was still time.

The aliens were coming. Coming to cap the climax of their pioneer work, to drive the first nail in humanity's coffin. For the first time in history man's dream of the brotherhood of man was close to reality.

And he was about to destroy it!

The irony bit into Matson's soul, and for a moment he hesitated, feeling the wave of tolerance and good will rising from the street below. Did he have the right to destroy man's dream? Did he dare tamper with the will of the world? Had he the right to play God?

The parade came slowly down the happy street, a kaleidoscope of color and movement that approached and went past in successive waves and masses. This was a gala day, this eve of world union. The insigne of the U.N. was everywhere. The aliens had used the organization to further their plans and it was now all-powerful. A solid bank of U.N. flags led the van of delegates, smiling and swathed in formal dress, sitting erect in their black official cars draped with the flags of native lands that would soon be furled forever if the aliens had their way.

And behind them came the Aztlans!

They rode together, standing on a pure white float, a bar of dazzling white in a sea of color. All equal, their inhumanly beautiful faces calm and remote, the Aztlans rode through the joyful crowd. There was something inspiring about the sight and for a moment, Matson felt a wave of revulsion sweep through him.

He sighed and thumbed the safety to "off," pulled the cocking lever and slid the first cartridge into the breech. He settled himself drawing a breath of air into his lungs, letting a little dribble out through slack lips, catching the remainder of the exhalation with closed glottis. The sights wavered and steadied upon the head of the center alien, framing the pale noble face with its aureole of golden hair. The luminous eyes were dull and introspective as the alien tried to withdraw from the emotions of the crowd. There was no awareness of danger on the alien's face. At 600 yards he was beyond their esper range and he was further covered by the feelings of the crowd. The sights lowered to the broad chest and centered there as Matson's spatulate fingers took up the slack in the trigger and squeezed softly and steadily.

A coruscating glow bathed the bodies of three of the aliens as their tall forms jerked to the smashing impact of the bullets. Their metallic tunics melted and sloughed as inner fires ate away the fragile garments that covered them. Flexible synthetic skin cracked and curled in the infernal heat, revealing padding, wire-like tendons, ropelike cords of flexible tubing and a metallic skeleton that melted and dripped in white hot drops in the heat of atomic flame—

"*Robots*," Matson gasped with sudden blinding realization. "I should have known! No wonder they seemed inhuman. Their builders would never dare expose themselves to the furies and conflicts of our emotionally uncontrolled world."

One of the aliens crouched on the float, his four-fingered hands pressed against a smoking hole in his metal tunic. The smoke thickened and a yellowish ichor poured out bursting into flame on contact with the air. The fifth alien, Ixtl, was untouched, standing with hands wide-stretched in a gesture that at once held command and appeal.

Matson reloaded quickly, but held his fire. The swarming crowd surrounding the alien was too thick for a clear shot and Matson, with sudden revulsion, was unwilling to risk further murder in a cause already won. The tall, silver figure of the alien winced and shuddered, his huge body shaking like a leaf in a storm. His builders had never designed him to withstand the barrage of focused emotion that was sweeping from the crowd. Terror, shock, sympathy, hate, loathing, grief, and disillusionment—the incredible gamut of human feelings wrenched and tore at the Aztlan, shorting delicate circuits, ripping the poised balance of his being as the violent discordant blasts lanced through him with destroying energy. Ixtl's classic features twisted in a spasm of inconceivable agony, a thin curl of smoke drifted from his distorted tragic mask of a mouth as he crumpled, a pitiful deflated figure against the whiteness of the float.

The cries of fear and horror changed their note as the aliens' true nature dawned upon the crowd. Pride of flesh recoiled as the swarming humans realized the facts. Revulsion at being led by machines swelled into raw red rage. The mob madness spread as an ominous growl began rising from the streets.

A panicky policeman triggered it, firing his Aztlan-built shock tube into the forefront of the mob. A dozen men fell, to be trampled by their neighbors as a swarm of men and women poured over the struggling officer and buried him from sight. Like wildfire, pent-up emotions blazed out in a flame of fury. The parade vanished, sucked into the maelstrom and torn apart. Fists flew, flesh tore, men and women screamed in high bitter agony as the mob clawed and trampled in a surging press of writhing forms that filled the street from one line of buildings to the other.

Half-mad with triumph, drunk with victory, shocked at the terrible form that death had taken in coming to Ixtl, Matson raised his clenched hands to the sky and screamed in a raw inhuman voice, a cry in which all of man's violence and pride were blended. The spasm passed as quickly as it came, and with its passing came exhaustion.   The job was done.   The aliens were destroyed. Tomorrow would bring reaction and with it would come fear.

Tomorrow or the next day man would hammer out a true world union, spurred by the thought of a retribution that would never come.   Yet all that didn't matter.   The important thing—the only important thing—was preserved.   Mankind would have to unite for survival—or so men would think—and he would never disillusion them.   For this was man's world and men were again free to work out their own destiny for better or for worse, without interference, and without help.   The golden dream was over.   Man might fail, but if he did he would fail on his own terms.   And if he succeeded—Matson looked up grimly at the shining sky…

Slowly he rose to his feet and descended to the raging street below.

THE END

If you've enjoyed this book, you will not want to miss these terrific titles…

ARMCHAIR SCI-FI & HORROR DOUBLE NOVELS, $12.95 each

D-61 **THE MAN WHO STOPPED AT NOTHING** by Paul W. Fairman
TEN FROM INFINITY by Ivar Jorgensen

D-62 **WORLDS WITHIN** by Rog Phillips
THE SLAVE by C.M. Kornbluth

D-63 **SECRET OF THE BLACK PLANET** by Milton Lesser
THE OUTCASTS OF SOLAR III by Emmett McDowell

D-64 **WEB OF THE WORLDS** by Harry Harrison and Katherine MacLean
RULE GOLDEN by Damon Knight

D-65 **TEN TO THE STARS** by Raymond Z. Gallun
THE CONQUERORS by David H. Keller, M. D.

D-66 **THE HORDE FROM INFINITY** by Dwight V. Swain
THE DAY THE EARTH FROZE by Gerald Hatch

D-67 **THE WAR OF THE WORLDS** by H. G. Wells
THE TIME MACHINE by H. G. Wells

D-68 **STARCOMBERS** by Edmond Hamilton
THE YEAR WHEN STARDUST FELL by Raymond F. Jones

D-69 **HOCUS-POCUS UNIVERSE** by Jack Williamson
QUEEN OF THE PANTHER WORLD by Berkeley Livingston

D-70 **BATTERING RAMS OF SPACE** by Don Wilcox
DOOMSDAY WING by George H. Smith

ARMCHAIR SCIENCE FICTION CLASSICS, $12.95 each

C-19 **EMPIRE OF JEGGA**
by David V. Reed

C-20 **THE TOMORROW PEOPLE**
by Judith Merril

C-21 **THE MAN FROM YESTERDAY**
by Howard Browne as by Lee Francis

C-22 **THE TIME TRADERS**
by Andre Norton

C-23 **ISLANDS OF SPACE**
by John W. Campbell

C-24 **THE GALAXY PRIMES**
by E. E. "Doc" Smith

If you've enjoyed this book, you will not want to miss these terrific titles...

ARMCHAIR SCI-FI & HORROR DOUBLE NOVELS, $12.95 each

D-71   **THE DEEP END** by Gregory Luce
           TO WATCH BY NIGHT by Robert Moore Williams

D-72   **SWORDSMAN OF LOST TERRA** by Poul Anderson
           PLANET OF GHOSTS by David V. Reed

D-73   **MOON OF BATTLE** by J. J. Allerton
           THE MUTANT WEAPON by Murray Leinster

D-74   **OLD SPACEMEN NEVER DIE!** John Jakes
           RETURN TO EARTH by Bryan Berry

D-75   **THE THING FROM UNDERNEATH** by Milton Lesser
           OPERATION INTERSTELLAR by George O. Smith

D-76   **THE BURNING WORLD** by Algis Budrys
           FOREVER IS TOO LONG by Chester S. Geier

D-77   **THE COSMIC JUNKMAN** by Rog Phillips
           THE ULTIMATE WEAPON by John W. Campbell

D-78   **THE TIES OF EARTH** by James H. Schmitz
           CUE FOR QUIET by Thomas L. Sherred

D-79   **SECRET OF THE MARTIANS** by Paul W. Fairman
           THE VARIABLE MAN by Philip K. Dick

D-80   **THE GREEN GIRL** by Jack Williamson
           THE ROBOT PERIL by Don Wilcox

ARMCHAIR SCIENCE FICTION CLASSICS, $12.95 each

C-25   **THE STAR KINGS**
           by Edmond Hamilton

C-26   **NOT IN SOLITUDE**
           by Kenneth Gantz

C-32   **PROMETHEUS II**
           by S. J. Byrne

ARMCHAIR SCI-FI & HORROR GEMS SERIES, $12.95 each

G-7   **SCIENCE FICTION GEMS, Vol. Four**
           Jack Sharkey and others

G-8   **HORROR GEMS, Vol. Four**
           Seabury Quinn and others

If you've enjoyed this book, you will not want to miss these terrific titles…

ARMCHAIR SCI-FI & HORROR DOUBLE NOVELS, $12.95 each

D-81 **THE LAST PLEA** by Robert Bloch
THE STATUS CIVILIZATION by Robert Sheckley

D-82 **WOMAN FROM ANOTHER PLANET** by Frank Belknap Long
HOMECALLING by Judith Merril

D-83 **WHEN TWO WORLDS MEET** by Robert Moore Williams
THE MAN WHO HAD NO BRAINS by Jeff Sutton

D-84 **THE SPECTRE OF SUICIDE SWAMP** by E. K. Jarvis
IT'S MAGIC, YOU DOPE! by Jack Sharkey

D-85 **THE STARSHIP FROM SIRIUS** by Rog Phillips
FINAL WEAPON by Everett Cole

D-86 **TREASURE ON THUNDER MOON** by Edmond Hamilton
TRAIL OF THE ASTROGAR by Henry Haase

D-87 **THE VENUS ENIGMA** by Joe Gibson
THE WOMAN IN SKIN 13 by Paul W. Fairman

D-88 **THE MAD ROBOT** by William P. McGivern
THE RUNNING MAN by J. Holly Hunter

D-89 **VENGEANCE OF KYVOR** by Randall Garrett
AT THE EARTH'S CORE by Edgar Rice Burroughs

D-90 **DWELLERS OF THE DEEP** by Don Wilcox
NIGHT OF THE LONG KNIVES by Fritz Leiber

ARMCHAIR SCIENCE FICTION CLASSICS, $12.95 each

C-28 **THE MAN FROM TOMORROW**
by Stanton A. Coblentz

C-29 **THE GREEN MAN OF GRAYPEC**
by Festus Pragnell

C-30 **THE SHAVER MYSTERY, Book Four**
by Richard S. Shaver

ARMCHAIR MASTERS OF SCIENCE FICTION SERIES, $16.95 each

MS-7 **MASTERS OF SCIENCE FICTION AND FANTASY, Vol. Seven**
Lester del Rey, "The Band Played On" and other tales

MS-8 **MASTERS OF SCIENCE FICTION, Vol. Eight**
Milton Lesser, "'A' as in Android" and other tales

If you've enjoyed this book, you will not want to miss these terrific titles…

ARMCHAIR SCI-FI & HORROR DOUBLE NOVELS, $12.95 each

D-91 **THE TIME TRAP** by Henry Kuttner
THE LUNAR LICHEN by Hal Clement

D-92 **SARGASSO OF LOST STARSHIPS** by Poul Anderson
THE ICE QUEEN by Don Wilcox

D-93 **THE PRINCE OF SPACE** by Jack Williamson
POWER by Harl Vincent

D-94 **PLANET OF NO RETURN** by Howard Browne
THE ANNIHILATOR COMES by Ed Earl Repp

D-95 **THE SINISTER INVASION** by Edmond Hamilton
OPERATION TERROR by Murray Leinster

D-96 **TRANSIENT** by Ward Moore
THE WORLD-MOVER by George O. Smith

D-97 **FORTY DAYS HAS SEPTEMBER** by Milton Lesser
THE DEVIL'S PLANET by David Wright O'Brien

D-98 **THE CYBERENE** by Rog Phillips
BADGE OF INFAMY by Lester del Rey

D-99 **THE JUSTICE OF MARTIN BRAND** by Raymond A. Palmer
BRING BACK MY BRAIN by Dwight V. Swain

D-100 **WIDE-OPEN PLANET** by L. Sprague de Camp
AND THEN THE TOWN TOOK OFF by Richard Wilson

ARMCHAIR SCIENCE FICTION CLASSICS, $12.95 each

C-31 **THE GOLDEN GUARDSMEN**
by S. J. Byrne

C-32 **ONE AGAINST THE MOON**
by Donald A. Wollheim

C-33 **HIDDEN CITY**
by Chester S. Geier

ARMCHAIR SCI-FI & HORROR GEMS SERIES, $12.95 each

G-9 **SCIENCE FICTION GEMS, Vol. Five**
Clifford D. Simak and others

G-10 **HORROR GEMS, Vol. Five**
E. Hoffman Price and others